THE NURSE AND THE CAPTAIN

It is 1918 and the Great War is ending. The evening before the last great battle, Ben hears that the flu epidemic has killed his entire family. Devastated, he is reckless in battle. Badly wounded, he is sent to an auxiliary hospital in England.

Laura's grandfather, the earl, has died, and she doesn't know what to do now. She volunteers at the local wartime hospital and is put in charge of a very sick officer ...

PHILIPPA CAREY

THE NURSE AND THE CAPTAIN

Complete and Unabridged

LINFORD
Leicester

First published in Great Britain in 2018

First Linford Edition
published 2021

*A catalogue record for this book is available
from the British Library.*

ISBN 978–1–4448–4726–0

Published by
Ulverscroft Limited
Anstey, Leicestershire

Printed and bound in Great Britain by
TJ Books Ltd., Padstow, Cornwall

This book is printed on acid-free paper

The Great War Draws to a Close

The briefing for tomorrow had been completed, dinner was over and now the officers were sitting around the officers' mess tent talking quietly.

They would shortly be returning to their units through the ever-present mud, but this was an opportunity to talk to fellow officers from other parts of the front line. There was more tension in the air than usual, as a big push towards the enemy lines was due early the next morning. A mess orderly was distributing mail that had just arrived.

'A letter for you, captain,' the orderly said, handing a letter to Benedict Richards, who was talking to his best friend, Jeremy Fellowes.

Ben took the letter and turned it over to slit it open with his finger. He paused as he read the return address.

'That's odd,' he said, continuing to open the envelope.

'Odd? What's odd?' Jeremy asked.

'It's from my father's butler — why would he be writing to me?'

Ben continued opening the envelope and with a frown took out the single sheet of paper. As he read the letter, his eyes widened in horror and his mouth dropped open. Finally his head dropped back and his eyes closed as he shook his head. The letter fell from his hand to the tarpaulin floor.

'No. No. This can't be,' he choked out, with his hands covering his face.

Jeremy only hesitated a moment before picking up what was Ben's private letter, to see what was distressing his friend so much.

My lord, I regret to inform you of recent events and must beg you to return as soon as possible, as we are in dire need of your advice and leadership. The estate and the village have been struck by an epidemic of what the doctor informed me is some type of virulent influenza.

I deeply regret to inform you that your entire family has been lost to us, with most of the younger staff members also passing away. I understand that the tenant farms and the village have been similarly afflicted and, as you know, they were already depleted by the young men who joined the war effort.

Many of the remaining workers have fled before they succumbed to the illness as well, so we now have only a handful of people to run both the house and the estate, many of whom are advanced in years. It seems unlikely the harvest will be taken in as the small community remaining will be fully occupied with livestock and the kitchen gardens.

I beg of you to return as soon as you are able, as we are desperate for your help and guidance.

Yours sincerely,
James Potter, butler.'

'Oh, Ben, this is just awful. How can everybody be gone so suddenly?'

Ben couldn't speak but just shook his head again as he sat with his hands still covering his face.

It was hard to imagine his parents, younger brother and both schoolgirl sisters had all been struck down. He had been hoping for some home leave next month, but what was the point now?

Jeremy stood and went across the room to speak to the adjutant. There followed a short conversation, during which they both glanced back at Ben, before Jeremy returned to Ben's side.

'I explained the situation to the adjutant and he'll arrange transport home for you tomorrow evening as soon as there's a lull in the advance.'

'Thanks. I'll get my batman to start packing right away,' Ben said in a dull voice.

He looked around. The atmosphere was sombre and the voices subdued.

Many of the men were writing letters that they would leave with the adjutant. However tomorrow's offensive went, some of the men wouldn't be back to

4

reclaim their letters and the adjutant would be sending them home to families with bundles of personal possessions.

There was no point in him writing such a letter as there was nobody to send it to now. Presumably his possessions would be sent back to the house, but whose house would it be?

Ben had a vague idea that after him and his brother, the heir was a distant cousin, but he really didn't know, and he had certainly never met him.

It hadn't mattered before, when he had a younger brother. If only his brother had been over nineteen years old and could have enlisted. Paradoxically, he might have been safer in the army — not that their father would ever have permitted him to join up as well.

It all seemed so futile. Fighting in the war had seemed, vaguely, a way to protect his family from the aggressive German Empire. Now he had nothing left to protect. His family was gone and the estate would soon be in ruins.

The older people left in the house and

on the estate would soon find they had no employment. Anyone too old for the army and too young for the minimal state pension would be in dire straits.

All he had remaining himself was his own life. He realised he was now Viscount Linton, not a title he had expected to inherit for a long time yet.

What value was there in being the fifth viscount? It was probably just a brief moment between the fourth and sixth, a tiny footnote in history of someone who never managed to accomplish anything. If he died tomorrow there was nobody to mourn him, nobody to remember him.

Perhaps he should make some futile but heroic grand gesture so that at least his name would live on in his regiment for a while.

Fat chance. Jeremy was likely to be the only one to remember him.

* * *

Very early the next morning the troops waited silently and nervously in their trenches. Previous offensives had been preceded by an artillery barrage, but this time there was nothing, the allies hoping to surprise the German troops.

A dense fog coated the countryside, further silencing the morning. Ben watched the hands of his watch slowly creep around to four o'clock.

He wondered if this offensive would be any more successful than the previous ones. At least this time they were pretty sure the Germans were weakened and the allies were bolstered by the Americans and Australians.

His shoulders sagged. Whatever happened, he didn't really care any more.

He would lead the way and in all probability would be shot, like many others, before going to join his family. Hopefully he could do something useful in the assault.

Suddenly all the officers studying their wristwatches blew their whistles and the men climbed ladders out of the trenches.

As they started across No Man's Land, the artillery barrage started up and the offensive was underway. The Germans were indeed caught by surprise by British soldiers looming out of the fog.

Ben and his men were most of the way across No Man's Land to the enemy trenches before the Germans started firing at them.

Ben saw a group of German soldiers gathering around a machine gun that would shortly start scything down his men.

'Rush that gun,' Ben shouted, and he led the way towards it, firing at the German crew with his revolver. He was nearly there when he was hit and fell face down into the mud.

Hampshire, Spring 1918

'Grandfather, it's time for your lunch,' twenty-year-old Laura Bascombe said to the frail and bedridden Earl of Spalding. 'Here, let me sit you up and get some pillows behind you.'

'I'm not hungry,' he grumbled.

'It's a very tasty oxtail soup,' she countered as she eased his shoulders forward and tucked a pillow behind him, 'and I know you like oxtail, so don't fuss.'

'I don't know why you bother, I'm not going to last much longer.'

'I bother because you're the only grandfather I have left and I have no intention of losing you any sooner than I must.

'Now eat it up and don't mess about, because I need to have my own lunch and get changed. We're expecting visitors this afternoon.'

'Visitors? I don't care who it is, don't send them up here, I won't see them.'

He drank a spoonful of the soup that

Laura offered him.

'Who is it anyway?'

'It's Mr and Mrs Waresley and Commander Waresley who is home on leave while his ship is in Southampton,' she said with a happy smile as she offered another spoonful.

'Oho! Commander Waresley is he now? Doing well for himself. Going to put your best dress on, I expect.'

He drank another spoonful.

'Well, I hope he offers for you this time. I thought he would last time before he was suddenly called to the Admiralty.'

He smiled.

'If he does offer, I suppose you must send him up to ask my permission, not that I shall refuse. And if he doesn't offer, you had better send him up to explain to me why not.'

* * *

After lunch, Laura put on a sky-blue dress that she knew suited her, before her maid Elsie brushed her hairuntil it shone.

She joined her aunt Cecily, Lady Bascombe, in the drawing room. Aunt Cecily was nominally in charge of the household, but in practice it was Laura, as Cecily couldn't cope with such a large house.

Cecily's son Daniel was Grandfather's heir and lived on another, smaller estate, Elmhurst Manor, not too far away. It was common knowledge, but not admitted to, that Cecily and daughter-in-law Mary did not get along. Thus it suited everybody for Cecily to live at Compton Park instead of Elmhurst Manor.

They heard the sound of voices downstairs in the entrance hall and Laura rang for tea. A few minutes later the butler came to the door.

'Mr and Mrs Gilbert Waresley, Commander Waresley and Mrs Horace Waresley.'

Laura glanced in confusion at Aunt Cecily. Who was Mrs Horace Waresley? Cecily looked just as confused. Then the awful truth dawned on Laura. Horace, her Horace, the Horace that she was proud of having been promoted to commander, the Horace she was expecting to marry, was already married.

This was not just a routine courtesy visit, this was to introduce the future mistress of the estate next door. When had they married? Why hadn't she heard about it? Was it when Horace had gone to the Admiralty during his last leave?

Laura was in shock and how she got through the next 20 minutes she couldn't recall. Fortunately, Aunt Cecily excelled at serving tea and making mindless chatter, so Laura didn't have to say much.

She cast a reproachful look at Horace, which he ignored, and then she realised she had no choice but to accept the situation for what it was. He had never actually promised anything and now his marriage was a fait accompli, so that was that.

The older Waresleys were blatantly proud of their son and his rapid promotion, and also of their new daughter-in-law, who was apparently the daughter of some senior admiral.

★ ★ ★

After their visitors had left, Laura made her way slowly up to her grandfather's bedroom. He was frail, but his eyesight was still good and his mind was sharp.

'Laura, where's Waresley and why the Friday face?'

'They've gone home and taken the new Mrs Waresley with them.'

'What?'

'He's married. He married his admiral's daughter.'

Her grandfather scowled.

'The bounder! How dare he lead you on and then do this. I shan't receive him if he comes calling.'

'You don't receive any visitors anyway.'

'Well, that's neither here nor there, I shall make a point of not receiving him.'

Laura smiled wryly.

'Is she pretty or ugly?'

Laura was not above a twinge of jealousy and derived some satisfaction when she replied to his question.

'She has a face like a horse.'

'Ha! More fool him. He'll have to live with horse face for the rest of his life. I expect the admiral was glad to get rid of her for the price of a promotion to commander. It does explain how he managed to advance so quickly. Are you very disappointed?'

'Yes, a little — it had been my expectation for so long. Perhaps it's for the best now he has shown himself to be so shallow.' A couple of tears rolled down her cheeks. 'My future seemed so clear and now ... '

'Well, he's stupid when he could have had you instead and he'll regret it one of these days. Goes to show he didn't care much for you after all, so good riddance to him. Were you in love with him?'

She took a deep breath and shook her head.

'No, not really. I had affection for him and I suppose it had become a habit

14

over the years to expect I would marry the man next door. No, I'll manage, it was just a bit of a shock.'

Her grandfather opened his arms and they embraced each other for several minutes.

'Don't you worry, my girl, be brave. I'm sure you'll come about,' he said, patting her gently on her back. 'Now I want you to go downstairs, find my worthless secretary and tell him to get up here straight away.'

Laura kissed her grandfather on his cheek and after finding the secretary, Mr Anderson, headed off to her own room to have a good cry for all her dreams and plans that had now crumbled into dust.

Last Wishes

A month later, Laura's grandfather was gone. One morning she had woken to a gentle knocking on her bedroom door. Her maid had opened the door to find a tear-stained valet saying that her grandfather had passed away in his sleep. Laura quickly put on her dressing gown and slippers before rushing to her grandfather's room.

'Oh, Grandfather!' she cried, hurrying to his side.

He looked as if he were just sleeping, but as Laura lifted his hand to her wet cheek, his hand was cold.

Laura sobbed her heart out. Her head had known for some time that he wouldn't live much longer, but her heart had not wanted to admit it.

After a while she felt a hand on her shoulder and turned to find Aunt Cecily also with tears running down her cheeks. They held each other tightly, finding comfort in the embrace.

Their anchor in life had gone for both of them and their future was now uncertain. Aunt Cecily had her son and his family to fall back on, but although Laura had aunts, uncles and cousins, she was not close to any of them. Her expected future had evaporated a month ago.

There was a discreet cough behind them.

'Excuse me, ladies, but the doctor is here and there are some formalities that must be observed.'

They nodded and headed back to their rooms to dress for the day. Laura's maid Elsie had known this day would arrive and she had prepared the black dress which she now laid out ready for her mistress.

* * *

Five days later, the funeral had been held, tea and a light lunch had been consumed and the family was gathered in the drawing room.

A table had been placed at one end of the room and a portly man, the late earl's solicitor, was severely dressed in black and standing behind it. He had wire-framed glasses perched on his nose and a sheaf of papers on the table in front of him.

The family were all dressed sombrely and they descended on the rows of chairs like so many rooks landing on a field. The servants all stood at the back, those not having black clothes wearing black armbands.

Daniel, the new earl, and his wife Mary sat at the front. His mother Cecily sat on the other side of him and next to her sat Laura. Laura and Cecily held hands.

In the row behind sat Laura's widowed aunt Agnes, Lady Weston, and her aunt's two daughters, Grace and Prudence.

Also in that row were Laura's other cousins, Ernest, Norman and Walter, with their widowed mother Aunt Phyllis, Lady Glatton.

Once all the family was seated, the solicitor also sat, cleared his throat and picked up the sheaf of papers.

'My lords, ladies and gentlemen, this is the last will and testament of Daniel Ernest Norman Walter Bascombe, the Right Honourable Earl of Spalding, prepared by myself a month ago and witnessed by two of my assistants.'

He paused and cleared his throat again as he lifted the sheaf of papers.

'I leave the following bequests to my faithful servants ... The entailed properties, principally Compton Park, are naturally to be inherited by my grandson Daniel, hitherto Viscount Bascombe.'

'My grandson Ernest, Baron Glatton, has often mentioned his love of the sea and sailing. It is, then, rather surprising he chose to join the Royal Artillery rather than the Royal Navy. To him I leave my yacht.'

A broad grin spread across Ernest's face. The solicitor hesitated a brief moment and appeared to be suppressing a smile.

'Not the one presently docked at Hamble, but the one upstairs in the nursery that I used to play with as a child.'

Ernest's mouth dropped open before he rose from his chair and hobbled as fast as he could from the room.

The solicitor paused for a moment as the remaining family looked at each other in surprise. When he had their attention again, and the door was closed behind Ernest, he continued.

'To my useless and good-for-nothing grandsons, Ernest, Norman and Walter, I leave two hundred pounds each with the hope that they use the money wisely and make something worthwhile of themselves.'

Norman and Walter looked at each other with raised eyebrows as the solicitor turned to the next page.

'To my daughter-in-law Agnes I leave the house in Littlehampton on condition that she live there for at least a year with her flatulent dog and two bickering daughters, so that the rest of the family are spared the noxious vapours and constant quarrelling.

'She may also have the benefit of my yacht in Hamble. My man of business has absolute discretion whether that is by leasing or selling the vessel.'

Agnes was frowning. This was good news and bad news. There were some quiet snorts of suppressed laughter from the front row.

'To my daughter Phyllis and daughter-inlaw Cecily I leave one thousand pounds each. In addition Cecily may have the use and income from the unentailed Elmhurst Manor estate for the next year.'

Daniel and his mother looked at each other with raised eyebrows. It seemed they were to exchange houses, at least for the next year.

'And finally to my granddaughter, Laura. I am conscious that she has spent a great deal of time being a welcome comfort and companion to me.

'Instead of caring for me she should have been getting married and starting her own family. I leave her five thousand pounds, require that she cast off her blacks immediately and go out and find a husband worthy of herself.'

Everybody looked at Laura to see her reaction but all they saw were tears rolling down her face and her hand being held tightly by her Aunt Cecily.

'That concludes the late earl's will for the time being,' the solicitor announced, 'but I ask you all to reconvene here a year and a week from now to hear the final disposition of the residual items, being principally money held in trust and the Elmhurst Manor estate.

'The will requests that before then, all the beneficiaries send me a report of their activities and achievements in the year starting now. The late earl has left me extensive instructions as to what final actions are to be taken based on those reports. Good day to you all.'

The family rose from their seats and started to drift back to the morning-room where refreshments had been set out. Laura and Cecily remained sitting down.

'This is all very well,' Laura said, with a frown creasing her brow, 'but now I don't know what I shall do. I'm at a complete loose end. He said I should cast off my blacks and find a husband, but I'm not in the mood to do either.'

'For a start,' her aunt said, 'why don't you come with me to Elmhurst? I'm sure Daniel will leave it in perfect order, but I will be grateful for your help and company. Perhaps we'll both find something useful to do.'

Laura was glad of the suggestion. She liked Cecily and it gave her a plan of action in the short term.

'Of course I will. Neither of us wants to get in the way of Daniel and Mary, so it will be a fresh start for all of us.'

'I expect Daniel will want to talk to the staff here and we can pack while he's doing it. Then we can all go to Elmhurst Manor together and he can make us known to the staff there.'

'He had better introduce us to the neighbours too, otherwise we shall be lonely, not knowing anybody.'

'Yes, he must do that, too,' Cecily said, nodding agreement. 'I must say it will be a relief to be in charge of a much smaller house.

'Between you and me, I've always found this huge edifice and the large staff rather daunting. As soon as we have settled in, we must look at your wardrobe and then find some social events to go to.'

The prospect of social events was not an inviting one for Laura.

'No, no, I'm really not in the mood for socialising at the moment. I just lost the man I thought for ages I would marry and then I lost Grandfather too. Grandfather was my guide for so long, I feel directionless now. No, we can go out later. Much later.'

'Remember what your grandfather said in his will. You are to cast off your blacks immediately and find a husband who deserves you. Staying at home feeling miserable will not do,' Cecily said, wagging an admonishing finger.

'Now, to practical matters. We shall obviously take our own lady's maids, but why don't we ask Anderson if he wants to come? He'll be at a loose end and Daniel is sure to bring his own secretary with him. Having a secretary of our own at Elmhurst could be very convenient.'

Laura looked at her aunt in a considering way. She was used to Cecily drifting along and leaving Laura to take charge. Suddenly her aunt was being very positive and taking charge herself.

Perhaps Laura had underestimated her all this time.

Settling In

Daniel and his family left Compton Park promptly in their motor car, the new Lady Spalding keen to set the changes in motion. She was eager to remove from Elmhurst Manor to her rightful place at the seat of the new earl, having been in expectation of the change for so long.

Laura and her aunt delayed their departure until the next day, so that all their belongings could be packed properly and being in no great hurry. They then followed to Elmhurst Manor in two of the old earl's carriages with their lady's maids and Anderson the secretary.

The war had taken their carriage horses, so they had to make do with some rather old farm horses. The new Lady Spalding wasted no time in introducing them to the housekeeper, cook, butler and steward, so before long they were sitting down to dinner.

'Mary, you must introduce us to some of the neighbours tomorrow,' Cecily said.

'Oh, there is no time for that, we shall be leaving in the afternoon. Besides, you have met the vicar, Reverend West. He and his wife will be calling in the morning to renew your acquaintance. They can introduce you to the rest of the local society, such as it is.'

Laura looked wide-eyed at her aunt Cecily, who sat with her lips pressed tightly and was obviously displeased.

'Cousin Mary, why is there such a hurry to go to Compton Park?' Laura asked.

'Why? To set things to rights, of course. With the old earl ill for so long and nobody properly in charge of the house, everything is surely sliding into disarray.

'Naturally, you will find everything here exactly as it should be, so there is no need for us to delay our departure.'

Laura was incensed. Whilst her grandfather may have been frail and confined to his bed, his mind had been sharp until the end and perfectly able to make decisions.

She herself had been quite capable

of running the household and since all of the senior staff were trustworthy and competent, everything was running well. Exceedingly well.

She opened her mouth to set her cousin right, when she caught sight of Aunt Cecily discreetly shaking her head. Laura understood and saw that starting an argument was a waste of time.

Since her cousins would soon be gone to Compton Park, she gritted her teeth and said nothing.

'Tell me, Mary, I have been reading about this organisation called the Women's Institute which has come over from Canada,' Cecily said, deciding to change the topic. 'Is there a branch here yet?'

'I believe so, but it's not for the likes of us.'

'Is it not? How is that so?'

'It's all to do with making jam and pickling vegetables. It's hardly work for ladies like us, is it? If you are curious, perhaps you should ask Cook.'

Laura could see this conversation was going to be fruitless, too, so applied herself to the food. Better to say nothing than lose her patience and say something she would later regret.

Now that Cousin Mary was elevated to the position of countess, she would not have much time for untitled ladies such as Laura or even for her dowager viscountess mother-in-law. No doubt she would credit herself and Daniel for the smooth running of Compton Park from the instant they arrived.

* * *

Early the next morning, Mary fussed around making sure that everything she wanted to take was loaded into the two old carriages which would follow them back to Compton Park.

Laura was fairly sure some of the items, such as an ornate writing desk, should have been staying at Elmhurst Manor. However, she kept quiet for the sake of harmony and told herself there was nothing of sentimental value.

As well, she and her aunt now had more

than enough money to buy replacements should they feel the need. She was more interested in seeing her cousins gone, so that she could have a little peace and quiet to sort out her bruised feelings and maybe make some modest plans.

The vicar and his wife arrived mid-morning and Carlton the butler put them in the morning-room.

He wasn't sure who the lady of the house was at that moment, so he informed both Mary and Cecily about the arrival of the visitors. As it happened, Mary, Cecily and Laura all arrived in the morning room together, which solved his dilemma, as he could simply announce them by rank.

'Lady Spalding, Lady Bascombe and Miss Bascombe,' he said before closing the door behind them.

The vicar bowed and his wife curtsied. Cecily and Laura smiled at them. Mary gave them a rather perfunctory nod which clearly said they were even further below her now than before.

'Good morning, Vicar, Mrs West,'

Mary said, 'I believe you have met Lady Bascombe and Miss Bascombe before?' She raised the corner of an eyebrow.

'Yes, indeed,' the vicar said, 'we had the pleasure of meeting them last Easter.'

'Good, good,' Mary said. 'I shall leave you to chat as I have a very busy morning. Good day to you.' Mary promptly turned on her heel and left the room.

Laura thought this was verging on rude, but she got the impression from the look on the vicar's face that it was no more than he expected. They all sat and Laura rang for coffee.

'We are very pleased to see you again,' Cecily volunteered, 'it seems ages since we visited and met you at church. I hope we shall see you both more frequently now that my niece Laura and I are going to be residing here.'

The Reverend West brightened at the news that his two new parishioners would be more sociable than those who were departing.

'I must say, Lady Bascombe, that you and Miss Bascombe are very welcome and I hope my wife and I can introduce you to some of the other families in the area.'

'Excellent. I was hoping you could introduce us to the local society. Do you have a Mothers' Union here, Vicar?' Cecily asked.

'Oh, yes, we do,' Mrs West replied. 'I run it and we meet every Thursday in the church hall. Currently we are very busy making socks, scarves and gloves for our soldiers in France.

'It seems very little that we do, but we try to bring some comfort to our men who are having such a horrible time in the trenches.'

'I shall be happy to come along and see if there is anything useful I can do as well. Perhaps someone could teach me how to knit. Is there also a Women's Institute in the area?'

'Oh, yes, they meet on Tuesday evenings, also in the church hall. They are making jams from the soft fruit that is in season now to send to the troops.

'I think your cook is a member of the

WI but she is often too busy here to attend the meetings.'

'I'm sure I can arrange for her to have a little more free time on Tuesdays,' Cecily remarked.

Laura thought that cousin Mary had been right about the cook, although she was sure it was a lucky guess more than actual knowledge. She couldn't imagine Mary being interested in the private lives of the staff.

'I don't know if it would interest you,' Mrs West added, 'but Walton Hall in the next village has been partly turned into an auxiliary hospital for wounded soldiers. They are always looking for volunteers, although I can understand it might not appeal to you.' Her tone then became more hopeful.

'I believe most of the men there are officers and some of them just need a little company to keep their spirits up.'

Laura's ears pricked up. Knitting and jam-making were not her style, but this sounded like something she could do.

She had experience of nursing her

grandfather and buoying up his spirits when he was down. Doing the same for wounded soldiers would be worthwhile and would give her a suitable occupation.

She was aware the Compton Park house and estate had been short of men due to the war, but she had done nothing to help the war effort directly. There had been little scope for ladies in her position and she felt a bit guilty at not having done anything.

'Mrs West, I think I might like to make enquiries about volunteering at the hospital. Do you know who I should ask for at Walton Hall?' Laura asked.

'I don't know, my dear,' Mrs West said, beaming at her, 'but I daresay if you ask for the matron, somebody will help you.'

After they had seen the Wests to the door and Daniel and Mary had departed with their entourage, Laura and Cecily returned to the drawing-room to sit quietly while they considered everything.

'Laura, I think I shall join both the

Mothers' Union and the Women's Institute. It will do me good to get out and see some new faces. Are you interested, too?'

'I think,' Laura said slowly, 'I would first like to investigate Walton Hall and see what they need. I'm not in the mood to socialise, but perhaps helping injured soldiers will give me a purpose.'

'Yes, dear, I think we both need something positive to keep us occupied. There's no point in dwelling on our grief when we could be helping others.'

'Quite right. I'm resolved to take the housekeeper's dog cart in the morning to Walton Hall. Also, now that Daniel and Mary have taken both carriages, we need something more than just a dog cart. I think it's time we got a motor car, too.'

'A motor car? Oh, dear. How does one go about getting one and who is to drive it?'

'I don't know, but I'm sure Anderson can find out.'

Short, Sweet and to the Point

In the morning, Laura's maid brought her a customary cup of tea and her usual cheery 'Good morning, miss.'

'Good morning, Elsie. I'm going to the army hospital at Walton Hall today. Apparently they need volunteers to help with the wounded soldiers, so I'm going to find out about it. A plain dress of some sort is probably most suitable.'

Elsie turned to the wardrobe and lifted out a dark blue day dress which Laura wore at home when not expecting visitors.

'How 'bout this one, Miss Laura? It's wool, so it'll be warm. There's a bit of a nip in the air this morning, I think autumn will be here sooner than we expect.'

'Yes, that's perfect.' Laura considered the visit as she drank her tea. She wondered if a chaperone was appropriate. Probably not, as the place was bound to be full of nurses, not just soldiers, although ...

'Elsie, I wonder if you might be interested in coming, too? You mustn't feel obliged to go and even if I volunteer to help there, you mustn't feel you need to volunteer as well. I really don't know what to expect and it might not suit either of us.'

Elsie stopped what she was doing, so as to think it over.

'Yes, miss, I would like to go with you. If nothing else, I'll see a bit more of the countryside around here.'

'Good. I can dress myself, so you go and change into outdoor clothes. I'll ask for the dog cart to be brought around while we're both having breakfast.'

★ ★ ★

By mid-morning they were at the entrance to the large and imposing Walton Hall to be greeted by the hall porter and a strong smell of antiseptic. He was using a crutch and missing his right leg below the knee.

'Good morning, miss, how may I help you?'

'I would like to speak to the matron if I may.'

'Certainly, miss, if you would take a seat in here,' he pointed to a small side room with his free hand, 'I'll go and find her. Who shall I say is calling?'

'Miss Bascombe. And Miss Dickens.'

They went into the side room and Elsie turned to Laura.

'You shouldn't be introducing me, miss,' she whispered, 'I'm just your maid.'

'No, Elsie, you're not my maid this morning. We're both young ladies who have come to see if we want to volunteer.'

Elsie bit her lower lip as she considered the idea.

Laura looked around the room. This must once have been the reception room for less important visitors. Now the carpet was rather worn and the furniture was basic and utilitarian.

A mature lady came into the room.

She was wearing a blue-grey dress with a short red cape and red facings to the dress. She had a white collar and a white muslin cap that looked a bit like a nun's hat.

'Good morning, ladies, I am the matron, how may I help you? Have you come to visit one of our patients?'

'I understand you are looking for volunteers,' Laura said, 'so we came to see what it's all about.'

'Ah, good,' the matron said, taking a seat. She cast an assessing look at Laura and then at Elsie.

'We do need extra help as the few trained nurses that we have here are overwhelmed with work.

'However, I should make clear right at the beginning the nature of the work of the volunteers.

'It's not case of taking tea with recuperating soldiers, although sometimes they do just want, or need, to talk.

'Most of the time you will be cleaning and carrying. Cleaning wounds, cleaning the men, cleaning the beds, the equipment, the floor, anything.

'Other times you may be carrying food to the men or carrying less pleasant things away.

'You will be working under the direction of a trained nurse and the two of you will be working in different wards.

'I realise this is not what you've been used to and some of it you will find distasteful or intimidating.

'If you don't feel you can both do all of it, then it would be best for us to part company now, otherwise we would be wasting each other's time.'

Well, Laura thought, slightly taken aback, the matron is outspoken and no fool. She's already worked out we are lady and lady's maid.

On the one hand she wants me to realise it's not a question of chatting over teacups. She wants me to understand and accept that the work may be dirty and demeaning.

On the other hand, she's realised that Elsie is my maid and won't have both of us in the same place and me getting her to do all the unpleasant bits.

Laura stiffened her spine. She wanted something useful to do, even if it would be hard.

'Thank you, Matron. I do understand. I've been nursing my recently departed grandfather for some time and appreciate some of what is involved with an invalid.

'As you can imagine, I didn't do everything myself, but I need something worthwhile to do, even if it is challenging for me. I am ready for it. How about you, Elsie? Don't feel you must, just because I'm going to.'

Elsie chewed her cheek for a moment.

'Please, Matron, what are the hours like and what would we wear?'

Trust Elsie to consider the practical aspects, Laura thought. It's just as well that one of us does.

'I think at first we'll keep you both just on the day shift, so eight a.m. to four p.m. with a break at lunchtime.

'You'll wear a light blue dress with a white apron and a handkerchief-style cap. You'll have two sets so that you always have a clean one when on duty. The trained nurses wear a different uniform so we can see easily who is who.'

Elsie nodded her agreement.

'Then, yes please, Matron, I would like to volunteer as well.'

'In that case I'll find one of the ward sisters. She will take all your details and give you uniforms in the right sizes. You should report, in uniform, to her at eight o'clock tomorrow morning. Welcome to the Voluntary Aid Detachment.'

The matron gave them a smile and swept away out of the room.

Laura and Elsie looked at each other with raised eyebrows. The interview had been short, sweet and to the point.

★ ★ ★

A little later they were on their way home in the dog cart with four uniforms stowed behind them.

'Well,' Laura said, with satisfaction, 'we'll be doing our bit from tomorrow. I suppose it is about time we got involved with the war effort.'

'Yes, miss, but there is something bothering me. If we're working at the hospital all day, when will I find the time to look after your clothes and so forth?'

Laura wondered if she really had given it all enough thought and chewed her cheek as she pondered how they would manage. 'Well, I will have to promote one of the chambermaids to be your assistant. I'll leave you and the housekeeper to suggest who it might be.

'Then each day you can tell her what needs to be done in your absence. We'll consider that you're training her to be a lady's maid and after a while you should be able to just let her get on with it. Mrs Bascombe's maid can lend a hand as well if she's not sure about something.'

Elsie frowned.

'But ... but what happens when the war ends and the hospital doesn't need us any more? You won't want two maids and she won't want to go back to be just a chambermaid, will she?'

'This is true, but how much longer

will the war last? In any case, I promise neither of you will be without a position. Who knows? You might have decided to become a trained nurse by then.' She grinned at Elsie.

Elsie chuckled at the idea.

'Nah! One my patients who needs a wife to push him around in a wheeled chair will have proposed marriage by then.'

They both laughed. The novelty and excitement of working at the hospital tomorrow had them in high spirits.

'I'll tell you one thing,' Laura said, 'I'm not going back and forth every day driving this confounded dog cart. The groom could take and fetch us, but this cart won't be big enough for three of us.

'My cousin hasn't left anything larger in the stables, so the groom will have to go and hire something for the time being. I'm getting a motor car but I'm not sure how long it will take.'

'A motor car?' Elsie breathed. 'Aren't they terribly expensive? And are ladies allowed to drive them?'

'Thanks to grandfather, I can afford one and whoever sells us it can teach me to drive. Perhaps he should teach the groom to drive it as well. The only thing is, I don't know anything about them or where you get them. I've already asked Anderson to find out.'

'You could ask the groom, too. The one what was driving the car has gone off to Compton Park now, but I 'spect he'll know something anyway.'

Laura nodded.

'Yes, you're right. In the meantime you had better tell the housekeeper you have my permission to steal one of her house-maids. Be sure to tell her, and the maid, too, that it's only temporary until we see how everything works out. She can hire a school leaver as a replacement.'

A Well-Earned Rest

As they left the hospital to return home after their first day of nursing, Laura let out a deep breath.

'I'm worn out! Nothing was particularly heavy, but it was non-stop.'

'You're not the only one,' Elsie said. 'You'd think I'd be used to it, but like you say, miss, it's non-stop. The only time we could sit down and get our breath was at lunchtime. Even that was rushed.'

'You know, Elsie, I don't think I've every properly appreciated how much you and the chambermaids do every day. Knowing the theory isn't the same as actually doing it yourself. Some of the smells and stains are pretty off-putting too.'

'I try not to think about the mucky bits.'

'Do you suppose it will be like this every day?' Laura asked.

'I 'spect we'll find out soon enough. There were more soldiers arriving today so that probably didn't help.'

'It said in the newspaper that there had been a big push in France and the Germans were falling back. If there was a big battle no doubt we'll be seeing a lot more wounded arriving.'

'If there's many more, I don't know where they'll put them. My ward is nearly full.'

'Mine, too. There can't be more than a couple of empty beds.'

'There must be men who are well enough to go home early and be looked after by their family and their local doctor,' Laura mused as she turned through the gates of Elmhurst Manor.

'Yes, we've got two in plaster with broken bones. I'm sure they could go home now. They'd have to be carried home, but that wouldn't be hard to arrange.'

'Who is my new maid? The lady's maid in training? I forgot to ask before.'

'It's Janet, miss. She was a chambermaid and she's right pleased to become a lady's maid, even if it's temporary.'

'When we get in, you can tell her I want a hot bath straight away. I have a lot of aching muscles and I fancy I can smell the hospital on me. Send Lady Bascombe's maid to show Janet what needs doing and what I'm going to wear this evening. Then you might want a hot bath too.'

Elsie looked at Laura with some alarm.

Laura laughed at the expression on Elsie's face.

'I just thought you might have aching muscles, too.'

'That's a relief, I wondered if I had a bad smell or had something on my face. Mind you, I'm not sure what they'll say about me taking an extra bath in the middle of the week.'

'If anyone grumbles, you tell them it's my instructions.'

As Laura swung the dog cart around the fountain at the front door, the groom came running around the corner from the stables to take it over. As they climbed down, a little stiffly, Laura turned to Elsie.

'You've done quite enough today, Elsie. Remember you're excused duties as soon as you've spoken to Janet.'

'Thank you, Miss Laura,' Elsie said, as she bobbed a curtsey and went back to being a maid.

'Excuse me, Miss Bascombe,' the groom said, before Laura went up the steps, 'I've been into town to look for a larger carriage, but there was very little available. There was a large governess cart that would take four people at a pinch and only need this single horse, so I took it. I hope that was all right?'

'I'm sure it will be. It's for you to take us to the next village and then bring it back in case Lady Bascombe needs it. It's only for a few days anyway. I hope to have a motor car soon and then we won't need it.'

'Very good, miss,' a relieved-looking groom said, touching his forehead before leading the dog cart away.

Laura wearily climbed the steps up to the front door held open by the butler.

'Carlton,' she said quietly, 'it has been a long, exhausting and grubby day for both myself and Elsie. I have instructed

Elsie to freshen up and take the rest of the day off.

'I expect you to quell any possible resentment among the other staff that Elsie is getting special treatment. She's not getting anything that hasn't been earned.'

'Yes, miss, I understand, I shall have a word with the housekeeper, too.'

'Thank you, Carlton,' Laura said and made her way upstairs very slowly.

* * *

Once Laura had refreshed herself and changed, Anderson came to find her and her aunt.

'I spoke to the chauffeur at Compton Park and he tells me they have a Rolls Royce Silver Ghost and gave me the name of the garage it came from. I then telephoned the garage.

'Unfortunately they don't have many cars to choose from, because production of private motor cars stopped at the start of the war so as to make vehicles for the war effort.

'However, they do have one in stock that might be suitable. It's five years old because it was manufactured before the war.' He referred to his notes.

'They say it is a Napier thirty horse-power landaulette which is in very good condition. They volunteered to bring it here for you to look at if you agree.'

'By all means,' Laura said. 'I have no idea what a Napier ... whatever it was ... is like, so we should certainly take a look.

'Tomorrow will be our second day at the hospital, and it will take us a couple of days to settle into the routine. Friday may be best, if that is convenient.

'Ask them if they can collect us from the hospital and drive us home. That way we will soon see if it is comfortable or not. In the meantime, the groom can take us in the morning and bring the carriage back, then collect us each afternoon.'

Anderson nodded and went off to make the arrangements.

Unwelcome Guest

The next day followed much the same pattern as the first, but Laura was glad to be collected from the hospital by the groom. It wasn't far to travel, which was just as well as there was little room to spare with three of them in the governess cart.

Nor was there any protection from the weather, which was starting to spit with rain. Laura and Elsie huddled tiredly under a large black umbrella that the groom had brought.

'I'm worn out again,' Laura said. 'I wonder if I will ever get used to it?'

'Yesterday was busy but today has been frantic, what with all the new arrivals.'

'Yes, I don't know where they'll find space. My ward is full and men that can sit or stand are getting moved out of the beds. I dare say many will be getting sent home today.'

'I thought it was a bit late for them to

be going home, but there were a row of cars and ambulances out the front.'

'I dread to think what is happening in France and how many won't be coming home at all.'

Both of them lapsed in a gloomy and thoughtful silence as the entrance gates to Elmhurst Manor hove into sight.

A few minutes later the groom drew the carriage to a halt at the foot of the entrance steps.

Now they were home, Laura and Elsie slipped back into their accustomed maid and mistress roles. Elsie followed Laura as they mounted the steps to the door being held open by Carlton. In the dim background Laura could see another figure.

'Captain Lord Glatton is here, miss,' the butler said as she entered the doorway.

'Ernest! What brings you here?' Laura said, going forward to receive a kiss on her cheek.

'I have come to see my favourite cousin, of course,' Ernest said, stepping back to survey Laura's nurse uniform. He glanced briefly at Elsie who slipped past on her way to the servants' door at the back.

'What's this?' Ernest asked. 'Going to a fancy-dress party?'

'Certainly not, and there's no need to be rude!' Laura said, frowning at him. 'I'll have you know I'm a volunteer nursing assistant at the local hospital.'

'My apologies,' Ernest said, looking astonished, 'but why? Why do you need to work as a nurse? Goodness knows grandfather left you enough that you don't need to seek employment.'

'Because, dear Ernest,' an irritated Laura said, 'I wanted to do something useful, so I volunteered at the army hospital. How are things at the Ministry of Munitions?'

'Very tedious, sitting at a desk all day, but infinitely better than standing in mud in Flanders.' He shuddered at the thought.

Laura had never liked Ernest. She gave him credit for volunteering for the army, but suspected he had been unwilling and pressured to join up by his friends. He had said at the time how everyone thought it would be over by Christmas, just when he would finish his training.

He had even admitted that his choice of the Royal Artillery was to keep away from the front line, but that it had stopped him being injured by enemy shell fire a matter of weeks after arriving in France.

She looked him up and down. He was wearing what looked like an expensively cut three-piece suit, shiny new shoes with spats and a vivid necktie.

'I see you have found time away from the war effort to visit your tailor. Now you must excuse me, I need to freshen up and get changed. I will see you later.'

'Ask my new maid to attend me,' she said to Carlton, before sweeping past her bemused cousin and heading upstairs.

The butler had a very straight face, before bowing slightly and heading for the servants' hall.

Laura reached her room, still fuming. That was typical of Ernest, she thought, he had always been self-centered and thoughtless. Fancy dress, indeed!

She didn't know why he had come but she doubted he would stay long. There wasn't anything for him to do here, with only herself and Aunt Cecily in residence.

She would be gone to the hospital in the morning before her cousin came down to breakfast and she couldn't imagine her aunt being entertaining company for him. With a bit of luck, he would be gone before she came home tomorrow.

Her new maid arrived and Laura busied herself getting changed into an evening gown. There seemed little point in donning a day gown when it would soon be time to change again for an early dinner.

She smiled to herself. Ernest would probably be surprised once more by how early they sat down for dinner. If she was going to be getting up again bright and early tomorrow, she would be going to bed early, too.

Laura went down to the drawing-room

to find her aunt and cousin sitting there with teacups in their hands. Neither of them looked particularly at ease.

'I say, Laura, Aunt Cecily says we dine at six-thirty — surely not?' Ernest said in shocked tones.

'Absolutely correct, dear cousin, I start at the hospital at eight o'clock in the morning, so we have moved everything forward a little.'

He looked at Laura, who was already wearing an evening gown.

'But, but … my goodness,' Ernest said, putting down his tea. He pulled out a gold pocket watch from his waistcoat pocket and looked at the time. 'If you will excuse me, I had better go and change right now.'

Laura and Cecily exchanged a grin as Ernest hurried from the room.

'He was a surprise when he appeared on the doorstep this afternoon,' Cecily said.

'I imagine so,' Laura replied. 'I was surprised, too. But why has he come? There's nothing for him to do here. Or has he forgotten that Daniel has moved to Compton Park?'

'No, I'm sure he knew that you were here.'

'Me?'

'I have a suspicion that his exceedingly modest inheritance has already been spent at his tailor and various entertainments in the West End. Who knows what else he might have been spending money on in the expectation of a bigger bequest from his grandfather? We all knew he had hoped to get the yacht, didn't we?'

They both grinned to recall the scene at the reading of the will. Neither of them had much fondness or sympathy for Ernest.

'But what has that to do with me?' Laura asked.

'I would guess that he is hoping to marry a rich heiress so that he can carry on as before.'

Rejected Proposal

Laura looked puzzled until the penny dropped.

'You can't mean me? Surely not?'

'I think so. You got a tidy sum from your grandfather, and for all we know, you might get Elmhurst too before the year is out.'

'Oh, no. It's all too ridiculous! He can't possibly suppose that I would marry him,' Laura said, giggling.

'Oh, but think of the advantages. You would be Lady Glatton and married to an elegantly dressed baron,' Cecily said, nodding with mock wisdom.

Laura snorted before bursting into laughter.

* * *

Ernest rejoined them nearly an hour later, dressed in a dark blue dinner suit and matching bow tie.

'My apologies for the delay, ladies, but

59

I didn't bring my valet and I have a devil of a time getting a bow tie just right.'

Laura viewed him with a raised eyebrow. Aunt Cecily looked him up and down.

'Blue, Ernest? A blue dinner jacket?' she asked.

'Why yes,' Ernest replied, preening a little, 'it's all the rage. Black is a little boring and dark grey has become quite unfashionable now.' He accepted a glass of sherry from Carlton.

'We must seem a little provincial to you,' Laura observed.

'Well,' Ernest said, pausing a moment as if he was trying to choose his words with care, 'these are the provinces, but no doubt the latest fashions will arrive pretty soon.'

'No doubt,' Cecily said dryly. She noticed the butler appearing in the doorway. 'Shall we go in?'

Ernest looked surprised that dinner was to be served mere moments after his arrival. He could only take a quick sip of his sherry before putting it down and following the ladies.

They went through to the dining-room where a small round table was laid for dinner. As there were normally only two of them to dine, it was more comfortable than the long table which could seat many more people.

The dessert finished, Cecily turned to Ernest.

'Would you like the butler to bring you the port bottle while we leave you to take tea?'

'Thank you, Aunt Cecily, but no. I was hoping to have a private word with cousin Laura, if I may.' He turned to Laura. 'Perhaps you could show me the gardens?'

They all stood as Laura and Cecily exchanged amused glances.

★ ★ ★

Laura and Ernest strolled across the lawns towards the flower-beds, Ernest walking slowly and stiffly due to his war wounds.

61

'This is a very pretty estate that grandfather left you,' Ernest said.

'Oh, no, you've misunderstood. It's not mine. He left it for Aunt Cecily to use for a year, then I expect it will revert to Daniel.'

'Why would he do that? No, it's clear that it will be yours at the end of the year. He probably did it this way to deter fortune hunters.'

Laura looked at Ernest quickly. The only fortune hunter that she knew of was walking beside her, if Aunt Cecily was correct, and Laura suspected she was.

'I'm sure you are wrong,' Laura said. 'I think he did it this way to give me a breathing space while I decide what to do. He knew Aunt Cecily wouldn't want to be at Compton Park with Cousin Mary any more than I would and he knew that we two rub along well together. I'm sure he fully expected Aunt Cecily to invite me to join her here for the year.'

'He also said you should not wear black and should get married.'

'Yes, but I'm not obliged to do so. As it

happens, I'm thinking of getting a small house in Winchester. It's an interesting city and not far from the family. He left me enough money to buy a house, invest the rest and live there with just a small staff.'

Laura decided to spin the tale a bit further.

'I would only need a cook, house-keeper, maid of all work and perhaps a footman. I could easily afford that. Then I'm enjoying the nursing and might volunteer at the local hospital. Perhaps I could get a dog or some cats, too.'

Ernest stopped abruptly and they faced each other.

'Oh, for goodness' sake,' he said, looking horrified, 'why would you do that? It all sounds terribly middle-class and bourgeois. It's not for the likes of you.

'And you shouldn't be mixing with all those sick people with working class diseases. Marry me and take your proper place in society as Lady Glatton. We rub along well enough, don't we?'

So, Laura thought, he didn't take long

to get to the point.

'It is kind of you to ask,' Laura said, 'but no, thank you. We wouldn't suit. Besides, what would we live on? You haven't come into your inheritance yet, have you?

'I don't suppose your allowance and your army pay come to much and I don't wish to live with your mother. Not that I have anything against her you understand, but neither of us would be comfortable.'

'There is this place,' Ernest said, sweeping his arm around to indicate the house and estate.

'But it's not mine,' she insisted. 'You have to believe me when I say I am just a guest here.'

Ernest studied her, clearly wondering whether to believe her or not.

'Look,' she said, 'ask Grandfather's lawyer. He probably can't tell you what will happen to Elmhurst but he might be able to tell you what will not happen. I'm quite sure he will tell you it's not going to be mine. Anyway, it's beside the point. I have no intention of marrying you or any of my cousins.'

'It's a great pity,' he said glumly. 'I thought it was a super idea.'

'It was good of you to think of me,' Laura said, 'but you need to find someone else. Now that you are so well dressed and working for the government in London I doubt you will have any difficulty drawing the attention of very many eligible girls.'

She privately thought his title would be an attraction in many wealthy families, never mind the rest of it. He didn't seem to be looking for someone to love, so it shouldn't be too hard to find some wealthy girl who would marry him.

Laura turned them both back towards the house and put her hand through his elbow.

'Now I need to retire early as I need to rise early in the morning and I don't suppose I will see you before I leave.

'By the time you've had breakfast, the groom will be back from taking me to the hospital. Why not get him to take you over to Compton Park?

'There's nothing for you to do here, but over there you could at least play billiards with Daniel or go for a ride.'

Laura didn't want to come home and find Ernest still here, ready with yet another hopeless marriage proposal.

A defeated Ernest let out a big sigh.

'Yes, I suppose that is the best idea.'

Laura patted his forearm, as if to reassure him that he was doing the right thing.

The Perfect Man

The next day, as they left Walton Hall on their way home, Laura could see Elsie was clearly bursting to tell her something but was restraining herself.

Once they had turned out of the short drive on to the road leading back to the village of Elmhurst and their house, the maid couldn't wait any longer.

'Miss Laura, I've found the perfect man for you!'

Laura was startled by the outburst and the horse hesitated, too, as the surprised groom jerked at the reins.

She turned to look at Elsie. Did she know of Ernest's proposal yesterday? The perfect man? What did she mean? Was her maid matchmaking now?

'It's a Corporal Mills,' Elsie said, rushing on. Laura had been assigned to a ward for officers and Elsie had a ward for noncommissioned officers.

A corporal? Laura thought. Whatever would Elsie think of next?

'Before he was called up he was a motor mechanic. When he joined the army they naturally made him the driver of a car for staff officers. Then one day a shell burst nearby, wrecking the car and killing the officers. He was thrown clear but had I don't know how many bones broken. He's still got a leg and an arm in plaster and he doesn't think he'll get sent back to the Front.

'Anyhow, I said you were thinking of getting a car and he asked me what kind. I said I didn't know. He said if you hadn't decided yet, he could offer some suggestions, if you would like him to.'

Elsie paused for breath.

Laura saw that Elsie had been chattering to her patients and was relieved she was talking about motor cars, not romance.

'Oh, Elsie, well done, that is a super idea. It would never have occurred to me to ask if any of the men had been drivers.

'I shall speak to him in the morning, but we'll have to come a little earlier. In my ward, Sister Hamilton is very strict.

She has a dim view of VAD nurses and only tolerates them because she desperately needs the help. She won't let me wander off in the middle of a shift.'

Laura was glad the groom was driving them home as she was once again worn out. They pulled up at the base of the front steps and the footman hurried down them to help her alight. Carlton the butler stood at the top holding the door open. As she approached him, he bowed slightly.

'Good afternoon, Miss Bascombe. The Honourable Walter Ramsey has arrived and is upstairs in the drawing room taking tea with Lady Bascombe.'

Laura's shoulders sagged and she groaned in a very unladylike manner, before deciding he would just have to wait a little longer.

'Very well. You may tell him that I have returned and I will join them in half an hour. No, make that three quarters of an hour. Send Janet up to me, if you please.'

Laura wondered what Walter wanted as she dragged herself up the stairs. If he had another marriage proposal like his eldest brother, he would get short shrift.

Somehow she doubted it. Ernest had always been self-centred and selfish. His brothers were different and she had always got on much better with them. Perhaps, she thought, it was an unfortunate side-effect of Ernest having been the heir and thus being treated more indulgently.

* * *

A generous 45 minutes later Laura appeared in the drawing-room to find Walter chatting companionably with Aunt Cecily. Laura was relieved to see that Walter was already wearing a sober black dinner suit and black tie. He bounded to his feet as she entered the room and came forward to kiss Laura on the cheek.

'Hello, Laura, you're looking very well and I'm glad to see you're not wearing black as grandfather instructed.'

'Walter, how nice to see you. How is Aunt Phyllis?'

'As far as I know, she is well, but I haven't seen her for the last week or so. Norman and I have moved out and taken lodgings in the City to be near our work.'

'Your work? You've taken employment?'

'Yes, I graduated this year and felt I needed something to do, not having much in the way of prospects, and Norman was tired of kicking his heels, too. We both joined a firm of stockbrokers called Schuster, Flywell and Schuster.'

'Goodness, that all sounds very industrious, respectable and what grandfather instructed you to do as well.'

'It does, doesn't it? I must say I'm enjoying it. And to be honest, that's why I've been sent by Mr Schuster to see you, Aunt Cecily and cousin Daniel too.'

'Oh. Sent by your employer? So you haven't come to propose marriage, then?'

'What?' Walter sat back, startled at the suggestion. 'No, certainly not. I don't want to get married. Not yet anyway, and probably not for some time. Not even to you, even though you're a splendid girl. Why do you ask? You're not in a certain ...' Walter blushed.

'No, I'm not in an interesting condition,' Laura replied hotly, 'and if you weren't my cousin I would box your ears for even asking!'

'Well, I ...' Walter blinked several times and stared at Laura with a puzzled frown.

'I'm sorry, that was unwarranted and unkind of me,' Laura said, rubbing her forehead, 'but I'm rather tired and feeling grumpy. Ernest came to see us only yesterday with the sole purpose of asking me to marry him.

'His pockets are empty and he had it in his head that Elmhurst Manor,' she waved her hands around at the house, 'was mine, which it's not.'

'I gather you refused him.'

'Absolutely. There is no way on earth I would marry Ernest.'

Walter nodded.

'I suppose I shouldn't say it of my brother, but he's totally irresponsible and I wouldn't want to see you married to him. Not that I mean,' he added hurriedly, 'that you're not a lovely girl and all that, but you would be all wrong for each other.'

There was a quiet pause as they all sipped the sherry that Carlton had served earlier.

'If anyone gets married in the near future, it might be Norman,' Walter said, grinning. 'Oh?' Laura asked with raised eyebrows.

Walter nodded.

'Soon after we joined the firm, we were invited to dine with Mr Schuster senior, the elder partner. He has a daughter of suitable age and I think Mr Schuster might like to see her married into an aristocratic family.

'Norman is the heir, at least for the moment, to the barony. If she married him there is a slim chance that she could become the next Lady Glatton.'

'What is she like?'

'She's no great beauty, fairly ordinary, really, to look at, but she's a very nice girl and has a warm personality. Of course, it must help her cause that her family is wealthy and her father is Norman's employer, too.'

'Do you think it will happen?'

'I don't know. It might. I thought I saw some mutual attraction. If you hear that Norman is changing his religion, then you will know.'

'Changing religion? Oh, I see, yes, I suppose I should have guessed from the father's name.'

'Phyllis would take a dim view of that,' Aunt Cecily remarked.

'I think she would soon get used to it,' Walter said, 'when she realises her son is getting wed to an heiress. She wasn't keen on us getting employment, either, until we pointed out that we had no choice but to find a salary. Not only that, but our clients were in the top layer of society.'

A light dawned for Laura and she sat up straight.

'Oh, I understand now. That's why you are going to see Daniel!'

'Precisely. I think that's why Norman and I got the jobs too. The firm is short-handed due to the war. I'm sure as soon as the partners saw that we were Right Honourables and Cambridge educated we were on the shortlist for interviews.

'On one level it seems dreadful and snobbish, but that's the way it works, I'm afraid, so we have to live with it.'

'Never mind. I'm glad you're finding your feet and you thought to call and see us, too.'

'Well ... ' Walter looked a bit sheepish. 'I have to confess that although I'm happy to see my favourite cousin and favourite aunt, my reasons are not altogether altruistic.

'You see, I happen to know you both came into some money not very long ago and the partners are quite convinced that the war will end soon. They say they have it on very good authority from someone in Whitehall, that the war will end this year.

'They expect the stock market to recover strongly as soon as it does. Consequently this might be a very good time to invest in stocks and shares.'

Laura smiled at Walter. She had always trusted Walter's judgement and she appreciated his being open with her. She didn't know what her aunt had in mind, but she certainly had cash sitting in the bank earning a poor rate of interest.

Laura hadn't given it much thought so far and she certainly wasn't really planning to buy a house in Winchester as she had pretended to Ernest.

One of these days she would have to make some sort of plan for her future, but in the meantime this sounded as if it might be a good opportunity that Walter had brought to her.

'That sounds very interesting, Walter. Why don't you tell us about it over dinner? If Aunt Cecily doesn't mind?' She turned to Cecily with a raised eyebrow.

'Oh, no, it sounds interesting to me too. I have no idea what will happen by next year so it might be sensible for me consider it, too. To be honest, I would welcome you or Norman helping me with advice. Daniel doesn't think his women-folk should be concerned with financial matters and I'm sorry, but wouldn't take any advice from Ernest.'

* * *

The next morning, Elsie took Laura straight to her ward to meet Corporal Mills. He had sandy curling hair, freckles and a cheerful expression on his face.

Laura thought he looked a bit young to have been at the front and wondered if he had lied about his age, as she knew it did happen. Glancing between him and Elsie, she also wondered if their mutual interest was more than just about cars.

'Good morning, corporal,' Elsie said, 'I've brought Nurse Bascombe to see you like I said I would yesterday.'

'Good morning, Miss Bascombe,' Corporal Mills said, ignoring the hospital protocol of addressing people by rank. He offered his left hand to shake since his right arm was still covered in plaster.

'Good morning, corporal. I understand you know all about cars.'

'No, not everything,' he said. He tried to shrug but it was difficult when you had an arm covered in plaster of Paris. 'In the army I was mostly driving officers in staff cars.

Before the war I was a motor mechanic in Southampton and we saw all kinds of motor cars then. What kind of car are you looking for? Something big for a family or,' he added with a cheeky grin, 'something small and sporting to cut a dash?'

'I think whatever I drive, people will think I'm cutting a dash,' Laura said dryly.

'You plan to drive it yourself then?'

'Oh, yes. Not all the time, but certainly when Elsie and I come here. I expect my aunt will use it for shopping or visiting, so then we'll need a chauffeur, too.'

He brightened at this news.

'I expect to be out of here in a few days, miss, and I doubt the army will want me back. If you'll be needing a chauffeur mechanic, I hope you'll remember me.'

'I'm sure I will,' Laura replied, thinking that if she didn't, she had a sneaking suspicion that Elsie would remember him for her. 'In the meantime, do you have any suggestions for what kind of car might suit me?'

'I dare say you could find something suitable made just before the war. A Vauxhall twenty-five horsepower or a Morris Bullnose should be readily available, easy to maintain and might suit you.'

Laura was impressed that he seemed to know what he was talking about, although it all meant almost nothing to her.

'As it happens, a garage is bringing a car here on Friday about four o'clock for us to see before driving us home by way of a demonstration. Perhaps you could take a look at the same time and give us your opinion?'

'I shall be pleased to, miss. What kind of car is it?'

'It's a ... ' Laura couldn't remember

and turned to Elsie for help.

'It's a Napier thirty horsepower landaulette,' Elsie said, looking pleased that she knew.

'Oh, very nice,' Corporal Mills said. 'They're very smart and good-quality cars, too. As long as it's been properly looked after it should suit you well.'

'Excellent. Thank you for the advice, corporal. I must get to my own ward now and leave you in the capable hands of Nurse Dickens. I shall see you on Friday, assuming you are up and about by then.'

An Aching Heart

Ben kept drifting in and out of consciousness. At one point he was being shaken up and down fairly violently. He was vaguely aware of the droning of an engine and it felt as if he was being driven fast down a very rough road.

What woke him and grabbed his attention was that everything hurt a very great deal and somebody was moaning. Was it him? A hand grabbed his arm and held it tightly, before relaxation spread through his body and he gratefully slid back to sleep.

The next time he woke up he realised he was on a stretcher being carried up a slope. The motion was causing his leg to knock against the side bar and it was excruciatingly painful.

'All right, captain, hang on, we'll be there in a moment and give you something for the pain,' a voice said.

The stretcher was put down and Ben felt a sharp scratch on his arm before he slipped back into oblivion.

Brief periods of waking with pain, hearing different sounds each time and feeling different motions left him very confused.

Finally Ben came slowly awake to the realisation that although his leg was still agonisingly painful, he wasn't being jostled about. It was fairly quiet, too, with a few footsteps and the murmur of voices.

He concentrated on the voices nearest to him in an effort to work out where he was and what was going on. It was hard to concentrate when his leg was so painful.

'Most of his wounds are reasonably minor, just keep them clean and bandaged. This gash on his calf is pretty bad, though, and has got infected. It will get septic if we're not careful so, Matron, you need to set up a Carel-Dakin drip straight away to sterilise it.'

'Yes, doctor. Should we continue with the morphine?'

'He's probably been on it too long already, so we'll switch him to laudanum.

That will be easier to reduce gradually over the next couple of days. You can give him aspirin, too. Once the infection is resolved we'll stitch him up. Call me at once if there are any concerns.'

'Thank you, doctor.'

A cool hand felt Ben's brow.

'Captain, are you awake?'

Ben forced open his eyes to find a motherly looking figure bending over him. She was wearing a nurse's uniform with a red shoulder cape. He nodded slightly in reply, but couldn't help wincing with the pain.

'Don't worry, captain, you're in the Walton Hall hospital now and I'm the matron. We'll look after you and get you well again. I'll be back in a moment with something for your pain.'

She straightened up and went away, leaving Ben staring at the ceiling.

This was all so stupid, he thought. Every day there were men dying in the mud in France. Men who didn't want to be there and whose families wanted them home.

Ironically, he, who had lost everything and had nobody waiting for him, was injured and sent back to England.

Why hadn't they left him to die in the mud, too? Instead he had been sent home to a hospital to get him well again. It was all so pointless.

Why, oh why, couldn't the Germans have killed him instead of someone else? Fate had a twisted sense of humour. Walton Hall hospital, she had said.

He remembered the house, more or less. It wasn't far from his home at South Dean. Had they brought him here to be near home? Ridiculous really, since home was now an empty house.

With an aching heart he remembered his parents, brother and sisters. All gone. He just felt empty inside thinking about them.

Many of his friends had died in the war, too, and the only one left was Jeremy. What had happened to Jeremy? Had he died in the big push or had he made it through?

He might be injured, too. Ben had no

idea and resolved to ask someone. There was a good chance he was all alone in the world now.

He closed his eyes and considered his leg. Perhaps it would get septic or gangrene and he would die. That would be best, if only it wasn't so painful in the meantime. It felt as if it were on fire.

'Sit up a little please, captain, and drink this down,' a voice said. He opened his eyes and saw it was the matron again.

'Drink it down and it will ease the pain.'

Ben needed no other inducement to drink from the cup, even though the liquid was bitter.

'Now have a little water to wash the taste away.'

Ben drank gratefully from a second cup, as he was thirsty.

'Captain Fellowes, let him know you're here before the medicine takes effect.'

'Ben, Ben,' a familiar voice said as a hand gripped his shoulder, 'you're in good hands now so I need to go and see my parents. I'll be back in a few days to see how you're getting on.'

Ben turned his head and looked blearily at the speaker. It was Jeremy, but wearing a bandage that covered most of his head and one eye. Thank God, Ben thought, Jeremy was alive even if he was injured.

'Jeremy,' Ben whispered. He tried to lift his hand, but he was too tired.

'There now, you have a little nap, captain, and as soon as the painkiller takes effect, we'll see to your leg,' Matron said.

Ben lay back, closed his eyes and was soon asleep again.

An Onerous Responsibility

'Nurse Bascombe,' a stern-looking Sister Hamilton said as soon as Laura arrived at the ward, 'I have an extra task for you today.'

Laura groaned silently. She had adjusted quickly to the busy routine of the hospital, but she was still worn out at the end of every day. She really didn't want any more work, but knew better than to say anything if she didn't want to feel the sharp edge of Sister Hamilton's tongue.

The sister was willing to accept the help of the upper-class girls who were members of the untrained VAD but she still held them in resentful contempt.

'Yes, Sister?'

'We had a new patient, Captain Richards, arrive yesterday evening and he has a wound on his leg that is not healing properly. It needs sluicing every two hours with Carel-Dakin fluid.

'You must make up the solution fresh

every morning with great care, as it must be made exactly in order to work properly.

'He needs almost constant attention and you will clean his wound every two hours without fail. Another nurse will take over from you for the evening shift. Do it properly and he may expect to keep his leg, get it wrong and his leg may need to be amputated even if the infection doesn't kill him.

'The doctor will look at the wound and measure the infection twice a day. It's regrettable that the wound hadn't been sterilised before he got here, but at least they got him here quickly, so I don't think gangrene has set in yet. Are you clear on all this?'

Laura was both shocked and pleased she was being given the task. Shocked because of the dire consequences if she didn't get it right, pleased because finally Sister Hamilton was entrusting her with something important to do.

'Yes, Sister, I will be very diligent and be sure to get it correct.'

'Good. I will teach you how to do it in a moment. However, there is something else. He was accompanied by a close friend, Captain Fellowes, who had a head wound in the same battle and so was free to come with him.

'He said to me in confidence that while Captain Richards was in France, he had lost his entire family here, every single one, to a virulent influenza epidemic. Thankfully we at the hospital haven't been struck by it.

'However, Captain Richards is depressed and suicidal as a consequence of losing everyone at home. That is the real reason Captain Fellowes has been staying close to his friend. He was afraid Captain Richards would do something rash and fatal, although he's been mostly unconscious so far.

'Now let me be very clear, Nurse Bascombe. I think suicide is ungodly and I will not permit it on my ward. Perhaps you think suicide is permissible when men have seen the horrors of war in the trenches?' Sister Hamilton studied

Laura carefully.

'Oh, no, Sister, I always think it is awful and must be very cruel to those who are left behind. I suppose in this case it may be different if he has nobody who would miss him. However, by the sound of it, he has at least one good friend who wants him to stay with the living.'

Sister Hamilton nodded at Laura's answer.

'Quite so. As I say, it is an ungodly act and I will not permit it. You, Nurse Bascombe, are to keep an eye on him and not allow him to do anything foolish. Nothing sharp or poisonous within reach.

'When he is well enough to get out of bed you are to keep an eye on him. If you can persuade him out of this frame of mind, so much the better, because we can't keep him here indefinitely. If he harms himself, Nurse Bascombe, I shall hold you entirely at fault, is that clear?'

Laura gulped. She was being made responsible for this man's life and for his mental wounds as well as the physical ones.

'Yes, Sister, I shall do my best, but it may be difficult if I am looking after all the other patients at the same time.'

'I understand that and will give most of your duties to the other volunteer on this ward. Now come with me and I'll show you what has to be done.'

★ ★ ★

Some minutes later they went to the ward, the sister carrying a bottle of fluid which she placed at the bedside of a patient lying there with his eyes closed. Laura had a waterproof sheet and fresh bandages and towels that she laid on the end of the bed.

'Captain Richards, this is Nurse Bascombe, who will be cleaning your wound every two hours until it is sterile and heals properly.'

His eyes flicked open and he gave them a tired look, his gaze lingering on Laura. He gave them both a small dismissive wave before closing his eyes again.

Sister Hamilton gently shook her head. 'I'll lift his leg while you take out the waterproof sheet and slide the clean one underneath.'

The sister then fetched a stand that had tubing hanging from it, before fitting the bottle of fluid.

'Now,' she said, removing the dressing on his leg, 'these tubes fit along the wound and drip the fluid into it. You put these dressings on top to keep everything in place.' She showed Laura what to do and looked at her for a nodded confirmation that everything was understood, before leaving her in charge.

Laura stood back and surveyed the bed and her patient. She would have to keep mopping up the excess liquid, otherwise everything would be soaked.

Her eyes travelled up her patient to discover a pair of hazel eyes looking at her from a rugged face with a heavily stubbled square chin. His hair was untidy and needed cutting. Tidied up he would be handsome. Now he looked scruffy, sleepy and exhausted.

* * *

Ben wasn't entirely sure what they had been doing to his leg. The painkillers were leaving him slightly fuzzy, but at least it didn't hurt more than it had done before.

The nurse — Nurse Bascombe, wasn't it? — was standing there looking at him.

Fortunately for him, they had had the kindness to give him a pretty one for his last days. He couldn't see her figure or hair due to the large amount of material in her uniform, but at least her face was attractive. She had brilliantly blue eyes that were studying him.

'Are you going to stand there all day staring at me?' he asked gruffly.

'No, Captain, but I shall have to keep an eye on the antiseptic and replenish it every so often.'

'There's no point. You should leave me and take care of the others instead.'

'What do you mean, leave you? We have to do this so your leg can heal. If it doesn't heal you'll lose the leg and might die from infection, too.'

'I'm probably going to die anyway, so it's a waste of everybody's time and energy.' He lay back on the pillow and closed his eyes. He felt worn out from talking.

'You are not going to die.'

'It would be better if I did. I'm just a burden and there is nobody to care if I do die, so I might as well.'

'Well, I care.'

He opened his eyes a crack. Her lips were pressed tightly and she looked as if she was on the point of bursting into tears.

'Nurse Bascombe, why do you care? There are men dying all the time. Don't say you've fallen in love with me already.' There was the suggestion of a sneer on his face that was otherwise grey with exhaustion.

'I loved my grandfather and he died only last month. I didn't want him to die, he was my rock, but now he's gone. Yes, there are men dying all the time and leaving their loved ones behind.

'You are able to live but you don't want to, you just want to throw your life away and all you can do is be sarcastic. Then, if you die, Sister Hamilton will say it's all my fault and I'll be sent home in disgrace.

'You're just an unfeeling ingrate,' she said with her voice cracking, before she put her hand to her mouth and walked briskly away down the ward.

Ben turned his head slightly and watched her hurrying away. He felt guilty. He hadn't meant to hurt her but he had. He was tired and bad tempered but that was no excuse.

Duty would undoubtedly bring her back soon and then he owed her an apology. Just because he was miserable, there was no need to inflict it on others.

He didn't do that sort of thing. His mother would have scolded him. But his mother was gone now, like everybody else, and as a fresh wave of anguish swept over him, he let sleep take him.

★ ★ ★

Laura reached the hallway outside the ward before she covered her face and let the tears roll. It was so hard. It was physically exhausting some days, but she could manage that. No, it was the men.

Some, like Elsie's Corporal Mills, were unremittingly cheerful, glad to be home and away from the Front. Some were worried, not knowing what was to become of them now they were crippled in some way.

Others seemed to know they were going to die and a few just lay there with blank expressions, as if their mind had gone for a long walk.

Now she had one who actually wanted to die and she knew it was because he had lost everything. It was the last straw and she couldn't deal with it.

She had done her best, but she wasn't suited to nursing. Looking after her grandfather hadn't prepared her for this.

She felt her face pulled on to someone's shoulder and a hand pat her gently on the back. After a moment she looked up and was surprised to see it was Sister

Hamilton.

'It's hard sometimes, isn't it?' the sister said. 'But you can do it. He needs us more than he realises and we have to be strong. Now dry your tears, blow your nose, stand up straight and go back in there. I'm confident you can do this.'

Laura did as she was told. She straightened up and took a handkerchief from her pocket. She wiped her eyes, blew her nose, nodded and went back into the ward.

It was going to be a difficult day. She had a fatalistic patient and a supervisor who was unexpectedly human. She would have to learn how to deal with both of them.

No Love Lost

Ben awoke at the feel of his leg being moved. It was Nurse Bascombe, back doing whatever it was she needed to do. He cleared his throat, ready to offer his apology and she looked up at the sound.

'I'm so sorry, Captain, was I hurting you? Would you like some more painkillers?'

'No, it's not that,' he said in a hoarse voice.

'Tea! You must be parched and want a cup of tea. The orderly came by while you were asleep and I said not to disturb you. Just a moment and I'll get you one.' She bustled off down the ward.

'No, I . . . ' Ben said feebly and flopped his head back on the pillow. This was frustrating. She should be angry, upset with him and expecting an apology, but she just wanted to give him tea.

She didn't deserve him and he didn't deserve her. Moments later she was back with a cup of tea and a small plate holding a couple of biscuits.

'Let me help you sit up,' she said, pulling him forward and pushing another pillow behind him, 'but try not to move your leg, it has tubes and things attached to it.'

'Nurse Bascombe, I ...'

She ignored his interruption.

'We mustn't disturb it at all if the infection is to be rinsed away.'

Ben was getting irritated. He wanted to be a gentleman and apologise, but he wasn't getting a chance. The irritation got the better of him.

'Nurse, it doesn't matter if the infection is cleared or not, it's all the same to me.'

'Nonsense. If the infection isn't stopped you will lose the leg.'

'It's not important, I will never walk again.'

Laura put her fists on her hips.

'Captain! Stop talking like this. I am determined you will walk out of this hospital. In fact, when you find a nice girl and marry her, you must invite me to the wedding and then you will dance with me.'

Ben looked at her as if she was losing her mind.

'You are being absurd.'

'Cousin Benedict,' a male voice said, interrupting them, 'good morning. I came as soon as I heard you were here.'

Ben squinted up at the man. He hadn't the faintest idea who he was and Ben was in a foul mood after quarrelling with his nurse. It was aggravating how she hadn't given him the slightest chance to apologise, so he didn't feel like being civil to this stranger.

'Who the hell are you?' he asked bluntly.

'I'm your cousin Claude.'

Ben blinked his eyes and stared at the man. The name meant nothing to him.

'Claude Legge. Your third cousin, once removed. Your heir.' Claude looked down his nose at Ben and waited expectantly.

Laura had found an upright chair and

placed it beside the bed, inviting the visitor to take a seat, which he did.

'I have just brought Captain Richards a cup of tea, sir. Would you care for one as well?'

Claude glanced at the tea on the bedside tea before giving Laura a small smile.

'Yes, thank you,' he replied and Laura went off down the ward again.

Ben frowned. He had a faint memory of a cousin Claude but never expected to meet him.

'Really? How did you find me? And why have you come?'

'After your family ... passed away and there was news that you were seriously injured, perhaps not to return from France, the family solicitor made enquiries.

'They were concerned that everything would fall apart in the absence of an heir, so I was sent for. In the meantime they heard you were here and let me know.

Consequently here I am, too.'

'You've wasted your time.'

Laura placed a second cup of tea next to Claude before moving away to give them some privacy.

Claude glanced at the apparatus surrounding Ben's leg.

'Have I? They expect you to live, then?'

Ben was still feeling grumpy and he decided he didn't like this Claude. He was skinny and badly dressed. He had a face like a weasel and greasy hair.

As well, he had a slimy demeanour to him and obviously had only come to see if he was going to inherit something.

It was not as if he was a close relative concerned about Ben's health. Ben had never even seen him before. Not only that, but it appeared he expected Ben to die.

No, Ben definitely didn't like this disagreeable stranger who had suddenly appeared from nowhere. He suddenly resolved to live, not die, so as to spite him.

'My nurse requires that I live. Anyway, there's nothing to inherit. I haven't been able to visit the house but a friend went to look.

'He says the only estate workers left are in their dotage and the crops are rotting in the fields. The animals have all been sold to pay wages and there's nothing left for repairs, so it's all going to rack and ruin.'

Jeremy hadn't said any of this — in fact, he had said almost nothing other than to let Ben know he was alive.

Nevertheless, it probably was more or less abandoned if there were no staff to look after it. He already knew from Potter, the butler, that most of the staff and tenants had gone, so it wasn't much of a speculation.

Ben wasn't going to tell this stranger that he honestly had no idea how things stood. No doubt everything needed attention and needed workers to give it that attention, but hopefully it wasn't really as bad as he was suggesting.

Ben hadn't cared until now, being ready to accept death and let whoever was his heir sort it out. Now he had met his heir, this Claude, he had changed his mind. He didn't want a chump like this inheriting.

'Perhaps you are plump in the pocket and can restore the estate?' Ben asked. He doubted it, because it didn't look as if Claude could afford a decent tailor.

'I afraid not, old boy, my pockets are empty. I would have to sell it all for whatever it would fetch. At least there is always the title.

'If I were Viscount Linton I could probably marry a rich girl which would sort it all out.' Claude grinned, seeming to be happy with his prospects.

Ben took deep exception to the man gloating over his expected inheritance.

'My executors would have to sell it all to cover my debts that are mounting. You would get almost nothing except the title.'

This was an outright lie. Ben didn't have any debts that he was aware of, but this Claude person couldn't know that.

He saw with satisfaction that Claude's grin had slipped. Ben wasn't dead yet and suddenly he was quite sure he didn't plan to be dead any time soon.

'Nurse!' Ben called. 'Nurse!'

'Yes, Captain?' Laura said, hurrying back. 'What is it?'

'I need to, you know … urgently … so pull the screens around and call the orderly, please.'

Laura pulled the mobile screens over.

'I'm terribly sorry, sir,' she said to Claude, 'but I'll have to ask you to leave.'

A slightly flustered Claude stood and picked up his hat with a trembling hand.

'Oh, very well, I'll come back in a day or two to see how you are getting on.'

Laura continued pulling the screens around the bed as Claude moved away.

'Psst!' Ben hissed to Laura who looked to see what he wanted.

'Yes, yes, sir, I'll be as quick as I can.'

'No, wait … ' Ben said quietly. 'Has he gone?'

Laura peeped around the screens to see Claude disappearing through the door at the end.

'Yes, sir.'

'Good. Don't bother with the screens,

I just wanted to get rid of him.'

Laura raised an eyebrow and looked at him in annoyance.

'Some patients realise how busy the nurses are and don't waste our time. I brought you both tea as well and now neither of you has even touched it,' she said in an exasperated voice.

'Sorry,' Ben said hastily and picked up his tea before she got even more annoyed with him.

'Ugh!' he said. 'This tastes foul, the milk must be off.'

'The milk is certainly not off,' she said with irritation in her voice, 'I have more sense than that.'

She picked up the second cup and tasted it.

'This tastes fine to me, it must be you.'

Ben was sure it wasn't just him.

'Taste this one, then,' he said pointing to his own cup.

Laura hesitated a brief moment before picking up his cup and trying it. She screwed her face up in disgust.

'It's foul, but I made them both the

same way.'

She and Ben stared at each other before Laura's eyes went to the side table where there should have been a small bottle of painkiller. It was missing.

'Who was that man?' she asked quietly. 'I've never seen him before but apparently he's my third cousin and my heir apparent.'

Laura's eyes widened.

'What?' Ben asked. 'What are you thinking?'

'You probably won't believe me but I suspect he just tried to poison you with your own medicine.'

Ben realised that she could be right. Was that why Claude was so cocksure about inheriting and then nervous when he went off?

'Well, I've missed an opportunity there, haven't I? I should have ended it all by drinking the bottle myself and saving both him and you a lot of trouble.'

'No, more fool me for leaving the bottle there. Rest assured I won't do so again,' she said, shaking her head at her own carelessness.

'Fear not, Nurse Bascombe. I have just changed my mind. I apologise for upsetting you earlier and I no longer plan to end my life because it would only upset you again. I find my cousin, Claude, completely detestable and don't wish him to inherit anything.'

Laura looked startled at his sudden change of attitude.

'Now I see my bottle of antiseptic hanging on the stand is empty. Isn't it about time you changed it? How will I ever get out of here if it doesn't heal?

'If you are not more careful I shall complain to the fearsome Sister Hamilton that you are not looking after me properly.'

Ben frowned comically at Laura and she grinned back at him. Ben felt his spirits lift. This Nurse Bascombe was not only very pretty, but she was very likeable too. He watched her set to work. He realised that he enjoyed watching her.

Now that he was planning to get well, she was someone whom he would like to know better.

He looked carefully at her hands as she attended to the drip. She wasn't wearing a wedding ring. Good. It would have been disappointing if she was married.

Ben wondered if she would stop to talk to him when she had finished setting up the apparatus. Then he suddenly felt guilty. No, it was all wrong. He should be in mourning, not with thoughts like this.

However, if the despicable Claude came back tomorrow he would need to enlist Nurse Bascombe's help to defeat his cousin.

Someone to Care For

Laura felt her mood lighten. If she was not mistaken, Captain Richards was shaking off his gloom. He had clearly taken a dislike to his cousin and that seemed to have galvanised him.

Now he was playing tricks on his cousin and bantering with his nurse. This surely had to be progress? Although she was a little shocked if he was going to move suddenly from deep gloom to light and chirpy. Didn't he have a family to mourn?

She didn't think he was on the verge of becoming hysterical, but she would have to keep a careful eye on him. It was going to be tricky to strike the right balance in her dealings with him.

However, regardless of his attitude, he needed to shake off his infection, too, otherwise it wouldn't matter one way or another.

She looked at his wound. She fancied that it was improved, but who was she to know? She carefully swabbed the area as she had been shown, ready to send the swab to the laboratory, before fitting a new bottle to irrigate the infection.

She stood and looked at the captain whose mind appeared to be elsewhere. His eyes turned to look back at her. She crossed her arms and mused about what might keep him thinking positively but not frivolously.

'Captain, you are a disgrace to the uniform.'

'What have I done now?' he asked in an offended voice.

'When is the last time you had a shave?'

He felt his stubble which was turning into a beard.

'I honestly couldn't tell you.'

'No, I thought not,' she said as severely as she could manage. 'It's time you became reacquainted with a razor, before the other nurses tell me I have the scruffiest patient in the hospital.'

He shook a reproving finger at her.

'Now don't you get any ideas about shaving me yourself. I doubt you have any idea how to do it and I would be covered in nicks. In fact, if you come near me with a razor, I shall seize it and cut my own throat.'

Laura was feeling a little smug. It seemed she had hit the right spot to get some animation back into him, which could only be good.

'Don't you worry, Captain, I won't give you a chance to do that. No, I shall go and find two strong orderlies to hold you down while I remove your beard.'

She strode off down the ward, trying not to look too pleased with herself and hoping that he was suitably outraged or horrified to see her going to find two orderlies and a razor.

A few minutes later she returned, followed by the batman who was looking after all the officers in the ward.

He was carrying a bowl of water in one hand, a towel over his arm and a shaving kit in the other hand. She nearly laughed to find the captain glaring at her with narrowed eyes.

'Now then, corporal, please do your

best to turn this shabby individual into someone respectable again.'

The batman looked uncertainly between the captain and the nurse.

'Begging your pardon, nurse, but he's like this because he wouldn't let me shave him before, not because I haven't asked.'

'I don't doubt it, corporal, but I'm going to stand here this time and make sure he behaves,' Laura said, crossing her arms again.

The captain and the batman looked at each other and Ben beckoned him forward with a slight movement of his head.

'You had better get on with it, corporal, or we'll both be in trouble.'

The batman put the bowl down and started making a lather with the shaving brush.

Laura watched with interest. She had never seen a man being shaved before. Her grandfather and his valet would never have let her watch what was a somewhat intimate procedure.

As the batman applied the foam to Ben's chin, cheeks and throat she found herself wondering what his skin would feel like when he was clean shaven.

The batman wiped Ben's skin clean with the towel.

'There you are, sir, good as new. I'll come back shortly and give your hair a trim, too. Don't worry, I can cut it so the graze across your head won't show.'

Ben nodded agreement to the haircut as Laura came closer. She knew she shouldn't do what she knew she was going to do, but she was his nurse and nurses were allowed to touch their patients, weren't they?

She put her hand on his cheek and felt his skin. She stroked her hand down and along his jaw.

'Much better,' she said.

He put his hand up and covered her hand, not to push it away but to hold it there. Their eyes locked. Laura didn't know what it was, but suddenly she felt a strong connection to this man.

Somehow, without reason, he had become her man, not just her patient, but her man to care for.

After all, she thought sadly, he had nobody else and everybody needed someone to care for them. She needed someone to care for, too. She determined to get him well and back on his feet, both literally and metaphorically.

Ben was surprised when she smoothed her hand on his jaw. It felt good to be comforted by another person, even if it wasn't quite what she really intended.

Yes, there was always his friend Jeremy, but it wasn't the same. Jeremy had a family and had to live his own life, and couldn't be supporting Ben all the time. Apart from Jeremy, Ben had nobody.

He put his hand over his nurse's hand to hold it there on his jaw and savour the moment. He held her gaze.

Perhaps, just perhaps, she cared about him a little and maybe just a tiny bit more than merely the professional care of a nurse for a patient.

The hope gave him a warm feeling somewhere inside that it might be so. He didn't feel utterly lonely any more. In fact, he felt the sudden need to get fit again. He couldn't die from this injury, because Nurse Bascombe would be disappointed in him and he didn't want that.

No, he saw her as a person now, not just one of the nurses. He wanted her to be happy. He turned his face and kissed her palm. She jerked her hand away and stepped back, looking flustered. Ben smiled. She looked adorable when she was flustered.

Laura wasn't sure what to do. She stepped back in surprise and alarm. Nurses shouldn't be letting patients kiss them, even if it was only their hand. Oh, how she would be embarrassed if anybody saw it, not to mention a likely reprimand ...

'Yes, um, well,' she stammered, 'it seems the batman has done a good job. He'll be back soon to do your hair.' She turned and hurried away down the ward.

Antiseptic fluid, she thought, yes, I should make another batch of antiseptic fluid. Antiseptic fluid mixing is good for calming the nerves.

A little later Laura returned to check on Ben's drip. He was napping, so she was able to study him quietly. Now that he was clean shaven and his hair was cut, she saw that her first impression had been correct, he was very handsome.

She had a little smile as she thought that having your hand kissed by a handsome man wasn't so bad after all.

A Helping Hand

The next morning saw a visit from Ben's friend Jeremy. Before going to find Ben, he asked for the matron.

The porter guided him down a hallway before knocking on a door.

'Enter,' a voice said and the porter opened the door.

'A Captain Fellowes to see you, Matron.'

'Good morning, Captain.'

'Good morning, Matron. I'm a friend of Captain Richards. I wondered how he was?' Jeremy asked anxiously.

'Ah, yes, I remember you from when Captain Richards was admitted.' She didn't say, but a tall army captain wearing a sort of turban covering half of his face was not hard for anyone to remember.

'I can tell you that the antiseptic treatment looks as if it is working and the doctor may be able to sew the wound closed very soon.'

'Excellent news, but I was more concerned with his mental state,' Jeremy said with a worried frown. 'He was pretty depressed.'

'Yes, I'm optimistic there, too. I've assigned a couple of nurses to him as he has needed fairly constant care. The ward sister says that one of them has managed to chivvy him into a more positive frame of mind.'

Jeremy was relieved at the news and relaxed slightly.

'Really? I must say that is encouraging. His personal circumstances were so dire that his depression was only to be expected. Frankly, I didn't know what to do with him.'

'Perhaps I could speak to the nurse before I go and see him? I wouldn't want to say the wrong thing accidentally.'

'Yes, of course. Wait here and I'll send Nurse Bascombe to see you.'

A few minutes later Laura came into the matron's office.

'Good morning, sir, Matron says you want to speak to me about Captain

Richards. How may I help you?'

Jeremy blinked. He hadn't considered what to expect, but if he had, this wouldn't have been it. She was exceptionally pretty and had shining hair peeping out from under her nurse's hat. Was this all it took to raise Ben's spirits? He concentrated on the task in hand.

'Matron tells me that Captain Richards' wound is improved and his mental state has improved, too.'

'Yes, that's right. The sluicing of the wound looks as if it's working and his mood seems lighter. I think the visit from his cousin annoyed him sufficiently that it jolted him out of his gloom.'

'His cousin?' Jeremy frowned as he couldn't ever remember any talk of a cousin.

'Apparently his third cousin and heir, a Mr Claude Legge. I understand he was almost gloating about the captain's imminent demise. His eagerness to inherit angered the captain sufficiently that it made him determined to live and cheat his cousin of any gains.

'And that's not all,' she lowered her voice to a whisper, 'we strongly suspect that he tried to poison the captain with his own medicine.'

Jeremy stared at Laura in amazement.

'What? No! That's horrifying! Has he been arrested?'

She shook her head.

'No, we can't prove what he did, although we're fairly sure. He said he would call again and I'll be watching him very carefully next time.'

Jeremy waved his hands disbelievingly.

'It's really stupid idea anyway, the estate is disintegrating. There's hardly anything to inherit. The farms are bereft of workers except for a few old men and the house has only the butler, house-keeper and one ancient gardener.

'The crops are not being harvested and will soon be rotting in the fields. The idea of attempted murder for such a damaged inheritance is crazy. Per-haps you've misinterpreted something or the cousin is either a fool or badly informed.'

Laura pressed her lips together in irritation at her idea being dismissed.

'Perhaps you had better come and speak to him yourself, sir. However, it might be wise not to talk about his estate disintegrating. I wouldn't want him getting depressed again.' She turned and led him down the ward to Ben's bed.

'Captain Fellowes to see you, sir,' she said and left them to it.

'Hello, Ben,' Jeremy said, as they shook hands. 'I hear you are on the mend and you do look brighter. I have to say, if I had a nurse as attractive as that I would be keen to get well too.'

'Jeremy, you mind your manners around Nurse Bascombe. She is a lady and deserves respect. She is hard working and taking good care of me. I'm very grateful to her and won't tolerate any impertinence towards her.'

Jeremy was taken aback at his friend's vehement defence of his nurse. Was there some undercurrent here that he had missed?

'Pax!' Jeremy said, showing his palms

in a submissive gesture. 'I have no ulterior motive, I'm merely observing that she is a decorative addition to the hospital which is just as well, as these places can be off-putting sometimes.

'I don't know why, but I half expected a grim Amazon of a nurse, so she caught me by surprise. I'm also a bit surprised about how fierce you are in her defence. Is there anything I should know?'

'No, nothing,' Ben mumbled.

'Fine,' Jeremy said, not really believing him. 'The nurse told me your cousin tried to poison you. What is that all about?'

'The scoundrel! While nobody was looking he emptied a bottle of laudanum into my tea. If it hadn't made the tea taste foul I wouldn't have known. Good job I was fully conscious by then and noticed.'

'Good heavens! I don't recall meeting any of your cousins. Has he always been vicious?'

'I have no idea, I'd never seen him before. The bottle of laudanum was on the side table — he didn't bring it with him. He probably thought I was in better shape than he had expected and seized the opportunity.'

'The nurse told me he said he'd be back soon.'

'No doubt he'll return to see if I'm dead or not. Forewarned is forearmed, so we'll know to watch him carefully next time.'

★ ★ ★

As Laura occupied herself with other duties, she recalled Captain Fellowes' comments about an estate. Captain Richards had an estate that was disintegrating, did he? And disintegrating due to lack of manpower? So now his depression made even more sense to her.

Not only had he lost his entire family, his estate was falling apart and by the time he was discharged from hospital, it would be too late to save it, so there would be nothing for him to go home to.

Well, perhaps she could do something about that. She had money. She had family and she had an aunt with a functioning house and estate. Surely they could lend a hand to keep the captain's inheritance above water until he got home?

She needed more of a purpose in life than just nursing patients and this might be it.

However, first she needed more information, so she waited and waylaid Captain Fellowes on his way out.

'Captain Fellowes,' she said, intercepting him as he left the ward, 'how did you find Captain Richards?'

'As you said, he is much improved. He also described his cousin to me in fairly derogatory terms and with a great deal of animation. It seems his cousin unintentionally did him a good turn by shaking him out of his lethargy.'

'I think you may be right. Tell me, what is the name of Captain Richards' estate and is it far away?'

'It's called South Dean, about ten miles south west of here. I suppose that's why they sent him to this hospital, as well as it being near the docks at Southampton.

'However, if they supposed it would make it convenient for his family to visit him, it's bureaucracy gone mad, because he no longer has any close family. Why do you ask?'

'My aunt has an estate nearby called Elmhurst Manor. It's where I live and why I volunteered at this particular hospital. I shall ask her this evening if she could provide a little help to keep South Dean going until the captain returns home.'

Jeremy regarded Laura speculatively for a few moments.

'Nurse Bascombe, I applaud your sentiments, but I fear that your aunt will already be shorthanded due to all the men who have joined the army. Indeed, I expect that many of her farm workers are not men but women.'

'Oh. I see. But I have to do something.'

He raised a questioning eyebrow.

'Do you? I wish you luck, but you may find it difficult. If I were you, I wouldn't say anything to Captain Richards. As you said before, I don't think we should let him know about the condition of his lands in case it demoralises him. Also, it wouldn't do to raise his hopes and then dash them again.'

'No, I'm sure you are right. Well, good-bye, Captain,' Laura said. 'Oh, wait. You said there was a butler. Do you know his name?'

Jeremy studied her for another long moment and then sighed.

'His name is Mr Potter and I warn you he is a bit old-fashioned. Good day to you, Nurse Bascombe.' He nodded to her and headed for the exit.

Laura felt sure there must be a way to help, but there was no point in arguing with Captain Fellowes, who was confident in his pessimism.

However, he had made a good point about saying nothing to Captain Richards. Even if she found a way to do something, his pride might be hurt if he thought a woman was saving his estate while he was stuck helpless in bed.

When she had a motor car it would be easy to take a look. Then she might have a better idea of what could be done, if anything. Waiting another day or so until she had a car probably wouldn't make much difference.

Transport of Delight

The following day was Friday and at four o'clock Laura and Elsie emerged from the hospital into the cobbled stableyard of Walton Hall, followed by Corporal Mills on a crutch.

They saw a man in a three-piece suit and bowler hat standing beside a very shiny motor car which had large brass lights at the front. It was dark green with gold and black piping around the doors and windows and looked very smart.

'Mr Hendy?'

'Yes. Miss Bascombe, I presume?'

'Yes, thank you for bringing the car to us. We need a car as soon as we can get one, but it is difficult to get away as the hospital is so busy.'

'It's no trouble at all. May I start by showing you the interior?'

Laura climbed in to see how spacious it was and to examine the button-backed upholstery in beige leather.

Meanwhile, Elsie went with Corporal

Mills around the outside so that he could inspect the bodywork and the tyres. Elsie was keeping an eye on him to make sure his crutch didn't slip on the cobbles.

'Mr Hendy,' the corporal asked, 'would you lift the covers over the engine compartment, please?'

The salesman promptly turned the bonnet catches and lifted the covers, confident that all would be in order.

'Would you like me to start the engine, sir?'

'Yes, if you would, please,' Mills replied, who then listened intently to the engine before nodding approval.

'Well, corporal, what do you think?' Laura asked, emerging from the back.

'Nothing wrong I can see with it, miss, without a closer inspection, which I'm unable to do at present,' he said indicating the plaster casts on his leg and arm.

'When do you expect to have them removed?' Laura asked.

'Pending a final examination, they said on Monday, miss. I'm looking forward to getting rid of them.'

'Very good,' Laura said, who was viewing the corporal as her likely chauffeur. 'I shall see you on Monday, in that case. Elsie, if you would help Corporal Mills back indoors please, while I speak to Mr Hendy. Then he can drive us home so Lady Cecily can take a look as well.'

A short while later they were driving back home. Mr Hendy was in the front while Elsie and Laura sat in the back.

'Coo, miss, this is a huge improvement over the governess cart,' a delighted Elsie said.

Laura couldn't help a smile at the awe-struck expression on Elsie's face. Elsie had clearly never ridden in a motor car before.

Even Laura had little experience of car travel, but Elsie was right. It was a very comfortable improvement over the governess cart or the dog cart.

Laura was already convinced that she was going to buy this car, whatever Aunt Cecily said. They would keep the dog cart for the staff and the groom would still be needed for the few horses.

Laura wanted to learn to drive, but she could see that having a chauffeur could be convenient too. Mills was the obvious man, especially if he was discharged from the hospital on Monday.

There seemed little point in trying to find someone else when he had all the experience she could wish for. She suspected that Elsie would approve.

When they arrived home, she asked Carlton to call her aunt to see the car.

'It looks very nice, dear, are you going to get it?' Aunt Cecily asked, having walked around it.

'Quite probably. It was very comfortable on the way here from the hospital and that road has a rather indifferent surface,' Laura said. 'Mr Hendy, perhaps you would step inside and we can discuss the details.'

Laura took him into the small front parlour before ringing for tea. Laura could easily pay the amount he was asking, but she had a shrewd idea that the price asked had increased as soon as Elmhurst Manor had been mentioned.

There was a short discussion about the price before they reached agreement. Well, Laura thought, it wasn't hard to get a reduction in the price and he looks cheerful, so it's probably the original price of the car.

'Very well, Mr Hendy, if you will excuse me for a moment, I shall go and get my cheque book.'

By the time she returned, he had completed most of the paperwork relating to the sale.

'Mr Hendy, I do realise it is too late today to present this cheque to your bank, but I am keen to get the car as soon as possible. What do you suggest?'

He looked at the cheque.

'I see your bank is a short distance from our garage. If you don't mind, I'll present it directly to your bank as soon as they open on Monday morning. I'm sure everything will be in order, so could I plan to collect you from the hospital again at four o'clock if that is acceptable?'

Laura thought that would suit her very

well, especially if Corporal Mills had been discharged by then. She knew she was going to be in a fever of excitement all weekend.

'Yes, thank you, Mr Hendy, that will be perfectly convenient.' She rose and opened the parlour door to see Carlton standing by the front door holding Mr Hendy's hat and gloves.

More Than Meets
the Eye . . .

On Monday, Mills had been discharged and promptly appointed by Laura to the post of chauffeur mechanic. Now he was sitting at the front with Mr Hendy who was explaining various details about the car as he drove it back to Elmhurst Manor.

Mills was to deliver Mr Hendy back to his garage once the ladies had been taken home.

As they drove home, Laura was wondering exactly where to find the captain's house. Once they arrived back at the manor, she called Mills before entering the house.

'Mills, have you heard of an estate called South Dean?'

'No, miss, I'm sorry, I haven't. Shall I make enquiries?'

'Yes, please do. It's our day off tomorrow and I would like to visit it. Perhaps the public house in the village might be a good place to try first for directions.' Laura's tongue was firmly in her cheek, guessing that Mills didn't need much of an excuse to visit the pub.

'I dare say there could be someone who's heard of it, miss,' Mills replied, trying and failing to suppress a smile.

Laura was reasonably sure there was a burgeoning romance between her driver and her maid. She also thought she might need their willing help tomorrow, so an exchange of favours might be in order.

'Elsie,' she said, turning to her maid, 'I won't need your help this evening but I daresay Mills might appreciate some help to question all the people. What do you say, Mills?' Laura winked at Elsie who instantly went bright pink in the face.

'I would say, miss, that I would appreciate Miss Elsie's assistance, if she is free and willing to help.'

'Well, I had been planning to wash my hair, Mr Mills, but since you asked so nicely I'm sure I could do that another time,' Elsie replied, pretending indifference.

'Good,' Laura said. 'You may take the car and since you'll both miss dinner at the house, I'll give you something to buy a meal at the pub.'

'Thank you, miss, that is very generous of you,' Mills replied.

'Now then, Elsie,' Laura said as she started up the steps, 'while Mills is taking Mr Hendy home, you will have time to change out of your uniform.'

At dinner that evening, Laura explained her plan for an exploratory visit to South Dean to her aunt.

'You remember what Captain Fellowes told me of Captain Richards' circumstances? I am concerned, aunt, about what may be happening, or rather, not happening, at South Dean.

'Captain Fellowes said the remaining staff are aged and there are too few of them to keep everything going.

'I plan to go and look tomorrow, expecting to find they need more workers to get the harvest in as a minimum. It's nearly the end of August and if something isn't done soon, it will be too late.

'Then there is the house which might not even be clean if the maids have gone. I think we should lend a hand to stop everything deteriorating further.'

'I don't understand, my dear. Why should we get involved?' Cecily said, creasing her brow in confusion.

'Because if he gets home and finds it has disintegrated in his absence, he might have a relapse. He was suicidal before and might be again.

'If we get him well enough to be discharged and then he kills himself it would be a disaster for everybody.

'All the people on his estate and working in the house would then feel deliberately abandoned, rather than just unfortunate. It would be a complete waste of all the efforts at the hospital, which is hard pressed as it is.

'Society is changing and those of us in a privileged position need to take a more constructive attitude to those around us. Furthermore, I would feel that I am complete failure if he harmed himself and so far I don't feel

I've achieved anything useful in the last few years.'

Aunt Cecily studied Laura thoughtfully for a minute or two.

'I dare say you are correct about the way times are changing, but you can't say you did nothing in recent years. You were a great comfort to your grandfather.'

'Yes, I hope I was, but it's hardly an achievement, is it? If I died tomorrow, it would be no more than a footnote in my obituary. Besides which, it made little difference to people outside the family.'

'Perhaps not, but have no doubt it was worthwhile. He would have been a lonely old man if we hadn't been there. As for Captain Richards, I'm not convinced we should get involved.

'For all we know, the captain might resent our interference. It might dent his pride that two ladies are trying to do what he was unable to do. He might get just as depressed if he feels inadequate and a failure.'

'You may be right, but letting him go

home to a desolation of his property and denting his morale simply can't be right. I think we need to help stop the estate getting any worse than it may already be.

'If he gets embarrassed or angry about us interfering, then it will be unfortunate, but better to be angry than depressed. I would rather be criticised for interfering than be criticised for doing nothing.'

Cecily looked fondly at Laura before sighing deeply. Her niece was animated and enthusiastic. She had been in low spirits after losing her grandfather and moving away from her home of many years at Compton Park. Now she was going to a lot of trouble on behalf of a particular patient at the hospital.

It seemed to Cecily that there might be more going on here than met the eye. As she understood it, the patient was a wounded officer who was apparently the owner of an estate comprising a house and an estate with several tenant farms.

Cecily would not be at all surprised if this Captain Richards was an eligible young man for whom Laura was developing tender feelings. This wasn't something Cecily had expected to happen when Laura volunteered at the hospital, but it was perhaps the sort of thing Laura's grandfather had been hoping for.

It was good she seemed to have forgotten the faithless Commander Horace Waresley.

Even if nothing came of helping this patient, Cecily was glad of the renewed vitality of her niece. She just hoped Laura's heart wouldn't be broken again, not that she really thought it had been broken before by Horace.

The Plan Comes Together

In the morning, Elsie came to find Laura at breakfast.

'Good morning, Miss Laura,' she said with a curtsey. 'We've discovered the whereabouts of South Dean, and Mills is getting the car ready.'

Aunt Cecily looked up.

'Will they be expecting you?'

'No, they won't be expecting us, but I thought it sensible to go have a look before we do anything else.'

'Perhaps I should come as well?'

'Yes, please, I would like another opinion. I wouldn't want to start doing something utterly foolish. Speaking of opinions, I should like to take Mr Jennings the steward as well, if he is free.'

When Laura had finished breakfast, she went to the estate office to find him and explain.

'Mr Jennings, I plan to go there this morning and see for myself how everything is. I would like you to come as well and give me your expert opinion on what needs to be done.'

Jennings looked flattered.

'Of course, Miss Bascombe, in your motor car, I suppose?'

'Yes, if you don't mind sitting in the front with Mills, my driver. Mrs Bascombe and Elsie will be sitting with me in the back.'

*　*　*

They arrived in the village of South Dean and stopped at the vicarage for Mills to ask for detailed directions to South Dean House. Half a mile further on they found a pair of tall black iron gates standing open and an entrance lodge that appeared to be empty.

The gravel drive was starting to sprout weeds. As they drove slowly towards the house, Laura and Cecily stared at it before turning and looking at each other in some surprise.

Elsie voiced their thoughts.

'It's a lot bigger than I expected. I

imagined it would be something like Elmhurst Manor, but this must be twice the size.'

South Dean House had a centre section of an entranceway with a pair of windows either side and it had three floors. Then there were wings either side which were three windows wide and two floors high.

The whole house had a service level at the bottom and there was a large, fan-shaped set of steps leading up to the front door. The whole house was of red brick with stone corners and stone window openings.

All the windows were covered with curtains, making it look abandoned. The lawns around the house had not been cut recently and the grass was getting very long.

Mills stopped the car at the base of the steps and everybody got out and looked around.

Mills went up the stairs and banged the knocker firmly. The sound echoed in the house but nothing seemed to happen.

Mills banged the knocker again as hard as he could while Laura went to stand beside him.

He was about to go looking for the servants' entrance or the kitchens when they heard footsteps.

The door creaked open and an old man peered out. He was dressed in tail-coat, striped trousers, waistcoat and wing collar. His clothes were a little creased and his grey hair needing brushing. One might speculate that he was a butler who had just awoken from a nap.

'Yes?'

Laura took a dim view of his appearance. It seemed to reflect the unkempt look of the house and the grounds.

'Good morning. You are Mr Potter, I presume?' Laura asked in a commanding voice.

As he heard her tone and accent, he straightened up.

'Yes, miss, I am. How may I help you?'

Laura had no intention of explaining herself on the doorstep. She pushed the door open and stepped inside.

'I am Miss Bascombe. This,' she said, waving a hand at the others, 'is my aunt, Lady Bascombe, Mr Jennings her land steward, and Miss Elsie Dickens, my maid.'

'I'm sorry, Miss Bascombe, but the master is not at home,' Potter said, looking annoyed.

'I well aware of that, Mr Potter. He is my patient at the hospital. You will probably be pleased to know that he is recovering and will probably be discharged before very long.'

'I am indeed pleased to hear that Miss Bascombe, but ... ' He looked around with frown, obviously wondering what was going on.

'Captain Fellowes tells me that the house and estate are in dire straits and we have come to see what needs to be done before Captain Richards returns. As I understand it, you are desperately short of manpower and everything is liable to collapse if something is not done at once.'

'Forgive me, miss, but I haven't properly understood your connection to my master. We had a recent visit from a Mr Claude Legge who I understand is the heir. He gave the distinct impression that he would inherit the estate soon, but there was nothing to be done as the estate was too far gone.'

'Did he indeed?' an outraged Laura said. 'You may forget that idea right now, Mr Potter. Captain Richards is recovering and neither he nor I have any intention of allowing Mr Legge to inherit. If he comes back I suggest you deny him entrance, at least until the captain has returned.'

The vehemence of her words made Potter take a step back and the others widen their eyes in surprise.

Laura decided not to explain her connection to Captain Richards any further, as she wasn't sure she could explain it to herself. She also realised that she was getting too worked up and should return to the point.

'As I understand it there is you, a housekeeper and a gardener. Are there no other staff in the house?'

'That is correct. This,' he turned to a plump older lady in a black dress who had emerged from the back of the house, 'is Mrs Green, the housekeeper.'

'I see. Is there no cook or land steward?'

'Mrs Green manages simple dishes for the two of us and the gardener. The land steward disappeared one day, taking all the ready cash with him. I informed the police, but I doubt they will find him.'

'The devil!' Aunt Cecily exclaimed. 'How could he do that when times are difficult?'

Laura cut across her aunt as they needed not to get sidetracked.

'How, then, are you managing for money?'

It was becoming clear to Potter that help had arrived and so he didn't prevaricate.

'With difficulty, miss. We have a little money saved and there are vegetables from the garden. The local shops have been extending credit as well.'

'Were you paid last quarter?'

'No, miss. We've been hoping the master will come back soon, take charge and sort everything out.'

Laura shook her head slowly in despair. The estate and tenant farms were probably in collapse as well.

'I shall have some money sent over tomorrow. Make a rough list of how much is owed to everybody and how much you need for the next month before we leave today.'

'But, miss, I don't understand ...'

'Never mind just now.' She waved him to silence. She was not going to clarify anything. She wasn't ready to do so, especially to the staff and she was far from sure exactly what she would be clarifying.

'Mrs Green, would you be so kind as to show Mrs Bascombe and Elsie round, please? We need to assess the amount of work needed to get the Captain's apartments ready for his return and probably a reception room, too.

'Mr Potter, would you come with me and Mr Jennings, please? We need to know where the tenant farms are and what needs to be done urgently. You can tell my driver where to go. I suggest we all reconvene here between one and two this afternoon.'

Potter and Mrs Green looked greatly relieved that somebody had arrived to take charge.

★ ★ ★

Later, nearer to two o'clock than one, they all sat around the kitchen table. Laura had the foresight to order sandwiches as they passed the pub.

They had stopped to collect them on their way back from visiting the farms, as obviously there would not have been enough in the house for lunch.

'I'll advertise for a cook on my return home,' Aunt Cecily said, 'and Mrs Green will see if she can find some girls who have just finished school this summer and haven't found work yet. They won't know how to do anything in a big house but they can soon learn.'

'We can loan a couple of elderly experienced men from Elmhurst and a couple of carthorses,' Mr Jennings added, 'purely on a temporary basis.

'Then Mills here,' he nodded at the driver, 'thinks he might be able to find some ex-soldiers who are not fit enough to go back to France but could make themselves useful on a farm.

'They'll soon learn you don't need two hands and two eyes to lead a horse or milk a cow.'

Cecily put her hand on Laura's arm.

'Are you sure about this dear? Hiring and feeding all these people is going to cost quite a bit of money.'

'Grandfather gave me more money than I know what to do with. I much prefer it to be spent on something useful than just sit in the bank. If Captain Richards is unhappy with it, he can consider it a loan until the estate is up and running again.'

'Miss Bascombe,' the butler said, 'I'm sure Mrs Green and the tenant farmers would join me in thanking you for your visit today. We've been very worried about what would happen to all of us, what with the family gone and the captain badly injured. You've set our minds at rest now, as it looks as if we shall all come about.'

'Mr Potter,' Laura said, 'I am happy to find something useful to do. Since my grandfather died and my aunt and I left Compton Park for Elmhurst Manor, we have also wondered what would happen to us too, so this could be considered therapeutic.

'Might I suggest you write a short note for the captain to reassure him that you are all coping, so as to relieve his mind? I want him to concentrate on getting well, not fretting about this place.

'I suggest you not go into any detail, especially about the absconding steward. Perhaps mentioning the school leaver maids and their low cost might be appropriate?

'Oh, and perhaps you could put together a small bag for me to take to the captain. I am hoping he will be out of bed

soon, so if he had his own dressing gown
and slippers, for example, that might be
nice for him.'

Reward for Bravery

It was mid-morning and Ben was sitting up in bed reading the newspaper when he noticed Nurse Bascombe hurrying down the ward towards him.

'Quickly,' she said, 'put that news paper away and let me straighten your bed.'

When he was slow to react, she whipped the newspaper out of his hands, folded it quickly and stuffed it in his bedside cab-inet.

'Hey, I was reading that! What's going on?'

'You've got important visitors,' she said, as she smoothed the sheets. 'Sit up.'

He obeyed the voice of command and obligingly sat forward while she patted and straightened the pillows.

'What sort of important visitors?'

'I don't know exactly, but they're in army uniform with red and gold bits on the hat and collar.'

Ben was surprised, because he hadn't

been expecting anyone, certainly not staff officers.

'Hmm. Must be at least a brigadier. What's he doing here?'

'I have no idea, Captain, but I think you are about to find out.'

A gaggle of men in uniform was coming down the ward, following the matron. Ben watched them approach, wondering what on earth was going on. Laura stood up straight with her hands clasped in front of her and moved to the side.

'Captain Richards?' the officer in charge said, offering his hand.

'Yes, sir,' a puzzled-looking Ben replied, shaking his hand.

'Well, you know why we're here,' the officer said and turned to accept a document from one of his entourage.

'Actually, no, sir, I have no idea,' Ben said, shaking his head.

'No? Didn't you get the letter?'

'Letter?'

'Ah. Obviously not. Well, never mind, I'm here now. I'm Major-General Seely, Lord Lieutenant for Hampshire. I'm sure you will understand His Majesty is very busy and unable to come all the way down here, while you are in no condition to go to Buckingham Palace.

'Consequently I am here as his representative with your citation,' he said, pointing to the document. He cleared his throat.

'It says here, 'The Military Cross has been awarded to Captain Richards for his act of exemplary gallantry during active operations against the enemy on the eighth of August 1918 near Amiens, France. He led a charge against a heavily defended German Army position with great speed and determination without thought for his own safety, so the position was quickly overrun.

''This saved the lives of many of his own men and was a material contribution to the large and rapid advance of the allied army that day.' Congratulations, Captain.'

The smiling general took the medal from his assistant and, after a slight hesitation, pinned it on Ben's pyjamas before shaking Ben's hand again. There was a round of applause from everybody who had gathered around his bed.

Ben was staggered, looking with a dropped jaw from the general to the medal, to the crowd and finally to Laura who was beaming with pride at him.

The general waited and everyone passed an uncomfortable moment of silence. It became clear that an astonished Ben wasn't going to say any more.

'Well done, Captain, you were an inspiration to the men around you. Well done, lad, well done, jolly good,' he said with determined cheerfulness before turning and nodding to the matron who guided the group back down the ward as the rest of the crowd dispersed.

'Congratulations, Captain,' Laura said. 'You must have been very brave.'

'No, no, it's not right,' a shocked Ben said quietly, finally finding his voice. 'They don't understand. I don't deserve this.'

He looked down in amazement at the medal pinned to his pyjamas.

'Captain, you are being too modest. The army obviously think you do deserve it. There must have been plenty of men who saw you and think you deserve it too. Besides, it sounds as if you saved the lives of many men.' She smoothed down the already smooth sheets.

'No, that's not it. You don't understand. It was only the evening before when I had learned that all my family had died and the estate was falling apart. I had lost everything. I wasn't being brave, I was being suicidal. I expected to die.'

There was silence as they both thought it over.

'You are looking at it from the wrong point of view,' Laura said. 'You chose to do something useful with your life for the sake of your men.

'It might have been reckless but as it happened it saved the lives of countless others. You made a choice and we all think you were very brave, even if your motives might have been suspect.'

'But I wasn't . . .'

'Yes, you were!' Laura insisted urgently. 'You might not believe it, but everybody else does. Now you've become an inspiration to them and you must not on any account disillusion them. Your real motive can be a secret between the two of us. Promise me?'

Ben reached up and took her hand which he squeezed gently as he nodded agreement.

'I promise, but there are times when I think the whole world has gone mad,' he said, 'then I wonder if I've gone mad instead. Just recently I've realised my only link to sanity is you.'

They looked into each other's eyes and Laura squeezed his hand back.

'That seems fair,' she said, 'because since I met you I gained a purpose in life.'

There was a cleared throat behind them and they dropped hands.

'Excuse me, sir,' the batman said, 'may I take your uniform jacket? I believe I need to add a ribbon to it now you are Captain Richards, MC.'

'I suppose you must, although I doubt I shall have much more cause to wear the uniform. I see from the newspaper the Germans are falling back rapidly. If it continues like this, it will all be over before I'm fit again.'

'That's a very welcome possibility, sir. They did say it would all be over before Christmas, but they didn't specify which Christmas, so perhaps it's this one.'

★ ★ ★

The day took another turn for Ben when a doctor appeared that afternoon to say that the infection had cleared, the drip could be dispensed with and he would be back shortly to stitch up the wound.

White Lie

'Your wound is healing nicely,' the doctor said next morning. 'You may now use a wheelchair, provided you have help from a nurse to get in and out of bed. I don't want you putting any strain on the muscle and tearing the stitches.'

'Thank goodness,' Ben said. 'It would be nice to get out and have some fresh air after so long.'

Laura came back ready to tuck Ben in again after the doctor straightened up from his examination.

'No, no, nurse, the doctor says I can use a wheelchair, provided you help me into it and I would really like to get out of this bed for a while.'

Laura looked at the doctor who nodded confirmation before moving on to the next bed.

'In that case,' she said, 'I had better find a wheelchair.' She stopped and turned back. 'It might take me a while to find one, so don't you dare move from

161

that bed until I come back,' she said, wagging a finger at him.

'Yes, miss, no, miss,' he said as meekly as he could.

Laura gave him a hard look, knowing that he was pulling her leg. She also knew that she not only had to find a wheel-chair but also find the bag that Potter the butler had given her.

She had left it in a store cupboard as she didn't want to tell the captain about their efforts to rescue South Dean House and estate. She wasn't sure how he would react. She feared he might see it as interference and get enraged, which was the last thing she wanted while he was recuperating.

A short while later she came back down the ward pushing a wheelchair that had a bag on the seat.

'What's in the bag?' Ben asked.

'Captain Fellowes told me about South Dean and I believe this is your own dressing-gown and your slippers, too.' She didn't want to lie, but she was happy for him to misunderstand and think that his friend had collected the items.

'Now, I'll pull back the bedclothes and help you swing your legs over the side. Then we can get you into your own dressing gown instead of the hospital one.'

Moments later, Ben was sitting on the edge of the bed wearing his own warmer dressing-gown. Laura had moved the wheelchair closer.

'Now,' she said, sitting next to him and putting her arm around his waist. 'Put your arm across my shoulder and stand up on your good leg. Then we'll turn and you can sit down into the chair.'

Ben put his arm across her shoulders but made no move to stand, instead turning his head to look into her face.

A puzzled Laura looked at him, wondering why he made no attempt to stand.

'Are you all right? Can you manage?'

'Oh yes,' Ben said blithely, 'it's just that it's rather cosy like this and I was enjoying it.'

'Captain Richards,' Laura said, feeling her face go pink, 'you are embarrassing me in front of the whole ward. Now please cooperate and concentrate, before we slip and fall.'

'Tumbling to the floor together could be interesting, too,' Ben remarked, still not moving.

'If I had a hand free, I would slap your face,' Laura hissed. 'Now move.'

'Oh very well,' Ben grumbled in a voice that was far from convincing. He stood carefully and half-hopped, half-turned, before lowering himself into the wheelchair.

Laura reached for a blanket to put across his lap.

'I've half a mind not to put your slippers on you,' she said quietly, 'it would serve you right to be punished with cold feet.'

'Oh no,' Ben said in mock terror, 'anything but cold feet. I'll do anything you say, nurse, but don't be so cruel to me.'

As Laura turned the wheelchair towards the end of the ward she swatted his shoulder. She was secretly very pleased that he was in such high spirits and ready to exchange banter with her.

She would miss him when he went home and she continued at the hospital with the other patients.

Shattered Dreams

Ben was now a regular visitor to the terrace on dry days or the reading room when it rained. Early in the morning he would be woken with tea and then the ward batman would visit to shave him. Next would be a visit from the doctor on his morning round before Ben transferred to a wheelchair.

An orderly would push him to the dining-room for breakfast and afterwards out to the terrace. There he would spend the morning chatting with other convalescing officers, reading the newspaper or playing cards. A similar pattern followed after lunch.

He was starting to get bored by the inactivity. He was also feeling conflicted. It was giving him too much time to dwell on his missing family. His head told him they were gone. His heart was struggling to accept it, as if they were still there, but he just hadn't seen them recently.

Making matters worse was Nurse

Bascombe. Now that he was no longer on the critical list, she had other patients that needed her attention while he was sitting on the terrace or in the reading room.

Yes, there were other officers to talk to, but it wasn't the same and when they went home, he would be left behind, alone and forgotten.

He missed her banter. He missed her chivvying him to be positive and look to the future. He missed her a great deal. He suspected he was falling in love with her.

During the times he could bring himself to accept that his family really were gone, he could see Jeremy and Nurse Bascombe were the only remaining bright spots in his life.

His cousin Claude didn't count as family as far as Ben was concerned, so his two friends were all he had. Were his feelings for her just gratitude and friendship?

No, he was pretty sure it was more than this, but he didn't know what she felt for him, if anything. Could it simply be a result of a kind professional attitude that she seemed warm and friendly towards him?

Ben knew it was necessary to take it easy while his leg healed but he wanted to get up and do something. By all accounts his house and estate were in a parlous state. They needed attention which he couldn't give from within the hospital. When he got home and reality set in, at least he would have a lot to keep him busy, so then he wouldn't have time to feel sorry for himself.

'Captain Richards?' a female voice said, jolting him back to the present.

Ben looked up. There was a plump mature lady standing in front of him dressed almost entirely in black except for a string of pearls and a spray of blue flowers on a wide-brimmed hat.

'Er, yes, I'm Captain Richards,' Ben said, wondering who this was.

'How do you do?' she said, extending her hand. 'I'm Lady Bascombe.'

'Oh, Bascombe as in Nurse Bascombe,

I suppose? Please take a seat,' Ben said.

'Thank you,' she said, pulling up a chair, 'Laura has told me a great deal about you, so I thought I would pay you a visit and meet you myself. I hope you don't mind?'

'Not at all. I'm afraid there is not a great deal to do here, so that days do drag a little and a fresh face is always welcome,' Ben said, mentally discounting his cousin.

'I hear you are making good progress. Will you be back on your feet soon, do you suppose?'

'Yes, indeed, I'm hoping to be given a crutch or a walking stick in a few days. Once I can hop about on my own I can get home and see what's going on and what needs doing. My friend Captain Fellowes went to have a look and told me it was all in a dreadful state.'

'Yes, I heard that too and also there were hardly any staff. That's partly why I came to see you. I help out with the Women's Institute and the Mothers' Union and we make things to send to the Front, but it doesn't seem all that much.

'When you are discharged I wondered if you might like to come and stay with us at Elmhurst Manor for a few weeks until you've got your full strength back.'

Ben sat up straight at this surprising offer.

'Elmhurst Manor?'

'Yes, it's where we live, it's not far from here.'

Ben frowned in thought for a moment. Bascombe? Elmhurst?

'Yes, of course, Daniel Bascombe! I hadn't connected the names. I haven't seen Daniel since before the war. I never knew him all that well, but we would come across each other from time to time. How is he?'

'Oh, he's fine. They've been married just over a year now and I have a fine grandson. Daniel has a darling little boy called Andrew — he's almost a year old,' Cecily said with a fond smile.

Ben suddenly understood the terrible, shocking truth. The lady in front of him was the dowager Viscountess Bascombe. Nurse Bascombe was actually Lady Bascombe and Daniel's wife and viscountess.

But wait a minute. She wasn't wearing a wedding ring, was she? Ben remembered the stains sometimes visible on the nurses' aprons. No, it wasn't significant. She undoubtedly removed her wedding ring before starting work as a matter of cleanliness and hygiene.

Had he been falling in love with a married woman? A married woman with a child and now her mother-in-law was inviting him to stay with them for a few weeks.

What had he done to deserve all these cruel twists of fate? He had started to hope he might have some sort of new future with his nurse and now all his hopes had crumbled into dust.

This lady was making an offer clearly born in kindness, but which would actually be a torture for Ben. It was impossible to accept, but she couldn't know why, and he would have to reject her gesture as gently as he could.

'Lady Bascombe, that is a very kind offer, but I couldn't possibly accept. I really must go to my own place and see what needs to be done.'

'Captain, there aren't the staff to look after you at South Dean and I'm sure you'll be much more comfortable with us.'

Ben gritted his teeth. He didn't want to be rude to this lady, but he must be firm. He would be horribly embarrassed and uncomfortable at Elmhurst Manor, so there was no way that he could accept.

'No, I'm sorry, Lady Bascombe, but it's quite impossible. I can't consider anything but returning to South Dean as soon as I may, as there will be so much for me to do.'

Aunt Cecily dithered and Ben wondered if she was going to persist. He hoped not.

'Very well, Captain, I shall leave you now,' Cecily said, rising from her chair, 'but I want you to consider my suggestion. I'm sure it would be best for your recovery and the offer remains open.

'If you should change your mind, don't be embarrassed and simply let Laura know so that we can make the arrangements.'

Ben knew there was absolutely no way he could change his mind.

Not to be Trusted

Ben was dozing again in the wheelchair which had been pushed out to the terrace. He had eaten lunch at a table in the fresh air for a change and the warm summer's afternoon had been lulling him asleep.

'Cousin Benedict,' a voice said, waking him, 'I'm pleased to see you must be on the mend if you are out of bed.'

Ben blinked himself fully awake to find his cousin Claude standing over him. Claude had a forced smile on his face which didn't reach his eyes and Ben had the firm impression that Claude was not at all pleased to see him recovering.

Ben recalled Claude's previous visit and the suspicious tea, so he was immediately on his guard. He looked around but his guardian angel in the form of Nurse Bascombe was not in sight.

'What brings you here, Claude?' Ben asked.

'Naturally to see how you are getting

on, as I don't suppose you have any visitors otherwise, do you?' Claude said, pulling up a chair.

Ben wondered if Claude was being deliberately crass in reminding him that his entire family was gone or if it simply came naturally. Either way, it didn't endear him to Ben.

'Where are you staying?' Ben asked, avoiding the question and determined to keep his temper.

'Oh, in Winchester. There's a tolerable inn by the river. I went to South Dean to stay there, but I was shocked to find you only have the housekeeper and butler there as de facto caretakers. When I asked for a bed for the night they said everything was under dustcovers, there was no cook and precious little food.

'Then there are weeds growing in the drive and the gatehouse looks abandoned. The lawns are all overgrown and the grass hasn't been cut for ages. I was glad the cab was still there. It all creates a very poor impression and the next owner will have a lot to do.'

Ben didn't care for Claude's tone, as if Claude thought the place would be his soon. Ben bit his tongue, determined to remain polite.

'Anyway,' Claude continued, as if he was talking to himself, 'I went back to Winchester.'

Ben was reaching the end of his tether.

'Since you have little to do, I wonder that you are still here. I am getting better, as you see, and surely it's time you went home?'

'Eh?' Claude said, returning to the here and now. 'Oh, well, yes I suppose I should be. I'll just leave you this,' he said handing Ben a half bottle of gin after looking around to see if anyone was looking. 'Put it under the blanket for now as I don't suppose they let you have a proper drink here.'

Ben looked at the bottle, instantly suspicious, before slipping it under his blanket.

'Very thoughtful of you, Claude. I'll have a nip when the nurses aren't looking.'

'Yes, you do that. Have a good swig in case they find it and take it away from you. Well, goodbye, old man. Enjoy the gin,' Claude said with a grin as he stood and shook Ben's hand.

Ben's eyes followed his cousin who was walking along the terrace, cane in hand, with what Ben thought was a slightly jaunty step. His eyes switched to Laura as she came in the other direction.

She glanced at Claude as they passed. He didn't think Claude noticed her. One nurse's uniform looked like another and Ben imagined that his cousin didn't even notice the staff unless he needed something.

Ben took the bottle out from under the blanket and looked at it carefully. It had already been opened as the seal around the stopper was broken.

'What do you have there, Captain?' Laura asked.

'I have a gift of a bottle of gin from my despicable cousin Claude.'

'I'm sorry, Captain, but the drinking of alcohol in the hospital is not allowed.

I shall have to confiscate it.'

Ben held up a staying hand.

'I suspect that this gin has been adulterated.' He removed the stopper and sniffed it.

'Here, you sniff it and tell me what you can smell,' he said, offering the bottle to Laura.

She sniffed carefully a couple of times.

'It smells of gin and ... almonds?'

Ben nodded.

'That's what I could smell too. There shouldn't be any almond smell, unless of course, cyanide has been added.'

Laura stepped back.

'Cyanide? Are you serious?'

'Deadly serious, if you will pardon the expression. He probably chose gin to add it to because gin has a noticeable smell of its own. What dear Claude has overlooked is that we are already suspicious.

'You would think he might wonder if we would be, after the previous unsuccessful attempt. Mind you, I did at first think the milk was off that time. Finally, what he doesn't realise, since he doesn't know me at all, is that I detest gin, so that was his worst possible choice.'

'Should I run and get him arrested by the porters?'

'No, don't bother. If he hasn't made a sharp exit by now, he'll just deny all knowledge of it.'

'We can't just let him get away with attempted murder.'

'We have to if we don't have solid evidence. In both cases there are no witnesses, so we can't prove anything. However, forewarned is forearmed.'

Laura looked at the bottle.

'What shall we do with this?'

'Don't pour it down the drain, we might kill the fish in the river or something. Slip it in your pocket, not to excite any questions, and take it into the garden. If you pour it at the base of a hedge it should be safe enough. Breaking the bottle 'accidentally on purpose' should discourage anyone from wanting to reuse it.'

'Is it that poisonous?'

'I don't really know, but it's best to be safe rather than sorry.'

Laura took the bottle and slipped it into her uniform pocket before walking off the terrace towards the shrubbery.

Ben sighed. He had come to depend on Nurse Bascombe. Not just as a nurse, but as someone he could talk to and look forward to seeing nearly every day. He was going to have to manage without her very soon.

There were a handful of staff left at home who would be familiar faces but it wasn't the same. They might be friendly but they were employees, not friends.

Then there were the missing faces of his family and other staff. The missing tenants would be just as noticeable. He was going to be very lonely.

So Far, So Good

Laura and her aunt Cecily were dining together in the evening.

'Has Captain Richards said any more about coming to stay?' Cecily asked.

Laura shook her head.

'No. I've tried to raise the topic a couple of times, but he's been very short in his refusal. He's due to be discharged tomorrow.'

'We can't just let him go home on his own. Rattling around in that place by himself he could easily fall into depression again.'

'That's what worries me. When he sees that we've had the place tidied up and the crops have been taken in, he might take it the wrong way, too.'

'You mean, see himself as not needed?'

'Exactly,' Laura said. 'No family to need him and then finding the house and estate don't really need him either.'

'I don't understand why he won't come here. Do you think it's a question of pride?'

'I don't know. He won't say why he objects to the idea. It will be on my conscience if he goes home and something happens to him.'

'We could kidnap him,' Cecily said calmly.

Laura dropped her dessert spoon on to her plate with a clatter.

'Kidnap? My goodness, did you just say we should kidnap him?'

'Yes, it's the only way I can see of protecting him from himself. Offer to drive him home instead of leaving him to be taken home by ambulance or whatever they do. Don't be specific about which home and then bring him to our home instead of his.'

Laura stared at her aunt. All these years she had thought she had known her aunt and now she had come out with this outrageous idea. But it might work.

'As soon as he realises what I'm doing, he'll refuse and demand to be driven home.'

'And you'll ignore him. What is he

going to do? Offer you violence? Jump out and run off on that gammy leg of his?'

Laura burst out laughing.

'Aunt, you have an evil streak in you. He's going to be so, so angry. He's going to be absolutely furious.'

The next morning Laura went first to the matron's office.

'Excuse me, Matron, but I need to speak to you about Captain Richards.'

The matron waved Laura to a seat.

'He's being discharged today, I believe.'

'Yes, and I'm worried about him returning to an empty house and getting depressed again, so my aunt has offered to let him stay as a guest for a few weeks while he recuperates.

'I would also like to remain at home for a few weeks to nurse him and make sure he is fit before he returns home.'

She paused, and the matron studied her thoughtfully.

'Nurse Dickens says that she wants to continue volunteering here during that period.'

The matron nodded slightly as she reached a decision.

'Very well, I think it is best for all concerned. You are both, of course, volunteers and as such free to leave whenever you want or need to. I have some patient discharge papers here to be completed.'

She handed Laura several sheets with forms printed on them.

'You need to fill in details of where he is going, and get approval signatures of the doctor, the patient and myself. He takes one copy with him and you leave the other two copies on my desk when he goes. Here, I'll do my signature now so you don't need to look for me later.'

As the matron was signing the forms, Laura wondered exactly how much she understood the situation and was simply turning a blind eye.

Laura picked up the forms as she stood.

'Thank you, Matron.'

'You take good care of him, Nurse Bascombe, and if you want to come back to us later, you will be very welcome.'

Laura left the matron's office, clutching the forms. That was the first part of the plan done. Now she needed to get Captain Richards' signature on the form without him realising that the destination address was blank.

Or, she thought, she could simply let him fill in the address of South Dean. It would make little difference because she was taking him to Elmhurst Manor regardless of what it said on the paperwork.

She supposed that the only time it would matter was if she got arrested for kidnap, so it would be best if he signed the blank form and she could put Elmhurst Manor before they left. That way he couldn't complain, could he? Oh, dear, Laura thought, I'm getting as devious as Aunt Cecily.

She went down the ward to find Ben dressed in his uniform, sitting on an upright chair and talking to his neighbour in the adjacent bed. There was a small valise on the floor and a walking stick hanging on the end of his bed.

'Good morning, Captain, I have your discharge forms here which will have all your details and just need to be completed. If you would sign them, I'll get the doctor's authorisation, too. After that you will be free to go and I'll arrange transport home.'

Ben took the forms and glanced at them.

'The destination is blank. I'll add the South Dean address as well.'

'There's no need. The transport driver will do that,' Laura said blandly.

Ben glanced at her. She seemed to be rather distant this morning. She was probably irritated by his refusal of her mother-in-law's offer. It couldn't be helped, it would be an intolerable situation.

It was best if this end of their association was to remain cool and professional. He signed the forms and handed them back.

'I'll be back shortly,' Laura said, taking the forms and his valise. As soon as she was out of sight she found a flat surface and filled in the address of Elmhurst

Manor.

Spotting the doctor starting his rounds, she seized the opportunity to get his signature. She left two forms on the matron's desk and put the third in her pocket. She then went out to give the valise to Mills, making sure the car was ready, before returning to the captain.

'Time to go, Captain. I'll take your arm. If you would take your walking stick, we'll make our way to the car nice and slowly.'

They made their way outside, the captain waving and nodding goodbye to acquaintances that he had made while he had been a patient.

'The hospital ambulance has had to go down to Southampton to meet more wounded off the hospital ship, so I've volunteered my car and driver to take you home.'

'That is a little irregular, isn't it?'

Laura shrugged.

'Transport is limited and you're not a patient any more, so it doesn't really matter, does it?'

'I suppose not, but it is good of you. I admit I don't want to stay in this place any longer than I must.'

They walked slowly across to Laura's car and Mills stood holding the door open.

'Good morning, Captain,' Mills said, throwing a smart salute.

'Good morning. Don't I know you?' Ben asked, looking at Mills closely.

'Corporal Mills, sir. Or I suppose I should say ex-corporal now.'

'Ah, yes, I remember now. No need to salute now you're out of uniform, is there?'

'Begging your pardon, sir, but I'm trying to be the best chauffeur there ever was.'

'Oh, I see. Well don't let me stop you,' Ben said with a grin. 'Carry on!'

'Thank you, sir. If you will pass me your walking stick, I'll help you inside before giving it back to you.'

Laura had hurried around to the far side of the car and climbed in. With her on the inside and Mills steadying him on the outside, Ben gingerly climbed up the two steps before sitting down on the back seat.

Mills passed the stick to Ben before closing the door and going to the driving seat. Ben noticed that Laura was sitting beside him with her door closed too.

'Are you coming as well?' he asked.

'Oh yes,' Laura said, nodding rather jerkily, 'it wouldn't do for you to fall over on the doorstep and have to come back, would it?'

'I suppose not,' Ben said doubtfully. He didn't think there was any need for her help. After all, there was the driver and when he got home there was his butler to lend a hand as well. Besides, he didn't feel unsteady and he didn't expect any problem.

He glanced at Laura. She seemed a little nervous and he wondered why. He was going to miss the young lady sitting next to him a great deal. He would have a lot of work to do and he planned to immerse himself in it, so that he didn't have time to think about anything or anyone else.

Attractive Proposition

Ben came out of his thoughts with a deep breath and a determination to look to the future. He looked up at the scenery as they drove down the road. It had been a long time since he had passed this way and somehow it seemed slightly unfamiliar.

They passed a crossroads and he glanced at the finger post giving directions. He blinked and realised they were going the wrong way.

'Stop, stop! We're going the wrong way. South Dean is in the opposite direction.'

He tapped his walking stick on the glass panel separating him from the driver. Mills slowed and glanced back. Laura flicked her fingers to wave him on and Mills sped up again. He already knew the plan.

Ben turned with a puzzled frown to Laura.

'You already knew we were going the wrong way, didn't you?'

'Yes, Captain, we are going to Elmhurst Manor where you will be our guest until you are properly recovered,' Laura said with a little smile.

'You wouldn't agree to the sensible course proposed by Lady Bascombe, so she suggested we kidnap you. I thought it was a jolly good idea and so here we are.'

Ben closed his eyes. These women were stubborn. Foolish, too. He had made it very clear that he didn't want to go to Elmhurst Manor. It would be torture for him to be with her constantly, and yet be polite to her husband at the same time. How could he explain without embarrassing everybody? He reached inside himself for his most severe officer personality and his voice was icy.

'Lady Bascombe, I must insist that you take me to my own house. When I call the authorities, they will take a dim view when they see what you have done. I cannot believe your husband agreed to this, either.'

Laura sat back and looked at him in

surprise.

'It seems, Captain, that you have several misunderstandings. Firstly, I am not Lady Bascombe, that is my aunt. I am Miss Bascombe. Secondly, I have no husband to agree or not agree, since I am not married.

'Finally, on your signed discharge papers, it says you are going to Elmhurst Manor, not South Dean. You may complain to the authorities as much as you like, but they will simply say that you agreed.' She handed him the form.

Ben was stunned and stared at her as he absorbed it all.

Laura giggled, then burst out laughing. Then she suddenly looked serious and put a hand on his sleeve.

'I said I would be taking you home, but I didn't specify which home, yours or mine. But I am very sorry, it must seem to you to be a wicked trick, but we were totally convinced that it is the best alternative for you. If we've gone too far, I apologise and I really will take you to South Dean instead.'

'Firstly, I need to get some things clear in my mind,' Ben said slowly. 'You say Lady Bascombe is your aunt and you are not married. So you are not married to Daniel and you don't have a son?'

She shook her head vigorously.

'Oh, no. Definitely not. Daniel is my cousin and although I quite like him, I would never have married him.'

'I see. But don't Daniel and his wife mind inviting a wounded soldier into their house for who knows how long?'

'It's not their house. They don't live there any more.'

Ben was confused again. Last time he saw Daniel he definitely lived at Elmhurst Manor.

'So where … ?'

'When my grandfather died, Daniel became the Earl of Spalding and they moved to Compton Park. Cousin Mary couldn't get there fast enough as the new Countess Spalding.' Laura shook her head slowly at the memory. 'Anyway, Aunt Cecily, Lady Bascombe, Daniel's mother, was granted Elmhurst Manor for a year and I moved there with her.'

'Why didn't Lady Bascombe stay at Compton Park?'

'Oh. She and the new Lady Spalding don't get on at all, I'm afraid. It's best for everybody if they don't live in the same house.'

'And your parents?'

'They passed away ten years ago. I had lived with grandfather ever since and nursed him for the last few years. When he was gone and we moved to Elmhurst I was very gloomy, at a loose end and I didn't know what to do with myself any more.

'Then I heard from some of our new neighbours about volunteering as a nurse at the hospital and here we are. Of course, I didn't realise then how difficult some of my patients would be.'

Ben smiled at her jest and at his new understanding too. His invitation to stay at Elmhurst wasn't as dreadful as he had thought — in fact it was sounding very attractive.

He was undoubtedly going to be

made very comfortable and, hopefully, cosseted by the pretty girl sitting next to him right now. His smile broadened at the idea and he looked into her eyes.

Laura was watching him carefully.

'Does this mean we are forgiven and you will come and stay with us for a while?'

Ben spread hands wide, palms up in a gesture of surrender.

'It seems I have been kidnapped and must give in as gracefully as I can. However this acceptance is conditional on you taking good care of me. Very good care.'

They sat back and Laura's hand covered Ben's hand. He clasped her hand firmly nearly all the way to Elmhurst Manor. An idea had occurred to Ben. As they slowed to enter the long driveway to the house, he turned slightly to face Laura.

'This kidnapping was Lady Bascombe's idea, didn't you say?'

'Yes, it was, what are you thinking?'

'I'm thinking I should pay her back

for her trick,' Ben said, who was now in high spirits.

'You have something in mind?'

'Yes, when we arrive at the house, we wait for her to appear at the door. Then you and Mills can pretend to drag an unwilling and loudly protesting man into the house.'

'That would be very naughty, but I like it,' Laura said, trying not to giggle again. 'When we arrive, let me get out first and explain to Mills before we begin the theatre.'

'Right. Just remember I have a gammy leg we must be gentle with, so don't pull too hard and I won't be resisting too hard, either.'

Confession Time

The car circled the fountain in front of the door, crunching over the gravel as it did so, before coming to a stop. The noise obviously alerted a waiting Aunt Cecily, since she appeared almost immediately at the front door. She stood there with a beaming smile and her hands clasped in front of her as Laura and Mills got out of the car.

Laura quickly said something to Mills as he opened the door for the captain.

'Come along, Captain,' Laura said in a very loud voice, 'it's no good resisting, we're here now and you must come inside.'

'I shall call the police! You can't do this to me,' Ben shouted as he stepped from the car. 'Kidnapping is illegal, I'll see you all in jail for this.'

Laura and Mills took an arm each while Ben leaned back slightly as if resisting.

'Resistance is futile, you must come

inside,' Laura said.

'Come along, sir, give in now,' Mills added in a carrying voice.

'No, no, I won't go,' Ben protested.

Aunt Cecily stood in the doorway, her eyes round with horror and her hands over her mouth.

'We can stop now, we've fooled her enough,' Ben said quietly, relaxing, standing straight and reaching for his stick.

Laura changed her hold from a grip on his arm to merely tucking her hand into his elbow.

'Lady Bascombe,' Ben said, 'thank you for your kind invitation, but I do think kidnapping was a little extreme.'

'Oh,' Aunt Cecily said, fanning herself with a hand. 'Oh dear, oh dear, oh dear.'

'Lady Bascombe, do forgive us if our playacting was too convincing, it was my idea to exact revenge, I do beg your pardon for distressing you,' a contrite Ben said.

There was a slight pause and then she hooted with laughter.

'Captain, you wicked man, you had me

very worried, but it was no more than I deserved. Welcome to Elmhurst Manor.' She stepped forward and shook his hand before they steadied him as he stepped into the house.

'It's a while until lunch,' Cecily said, 'so let us have some coffee on the meantime.'

They went into the small reception room on the ground floor to save the captain from negotiating the stairs just yet. Ben chose to sit in an upright chair as that was easier for him to get into and out of, while the ladies sat on the sofa. The butler circulated with the coffee pot and cream jug.

'Captain,' Laura said, once they were all served, 'before we go much further, there is more for us to confess.'

Ben raised his eyebrows but said nothing as he wondered what else they had done.

'I may be wrong, but I think you don't have a valet or batman at present, do you?'

'Yes, that's correct — but I have done

199

for myself more than once before.'

'Be that as it may, I have asked my late grandfather's valet to come out of retirement on a temporary basis.

'When grandfather passed away, Thompson was well provided for and retired rather than seek another post. I've asked him to valet for you until you make some other arrangement and, to be frank, I think he was bored and glad to join us.

'I'll introduce you shortly. If it doesn't suit you, just say and he can go back into retirement, at least knowing that he hadn't been forgotten.'

Ben wasn't sure that he wanted to add a non-essential person to his staff at the moment, but it would undoubtedly be convenient in the short term. Besides, if was understood to be a temporary arrangement, it would be easy to end it without embarrassment, if Ben either couldn't afford him or didn't take to him.

'Thank you, I'm sure he will be very helpful while my leg is still bandaged.'

'Before we go for lunch,' Cecily said,

'I imagine you will both want to change out of your uniforms. If you have finished your coffees, I'll call Thompson to assist you to your room, captain.'

'My civilian clothes are here?'

'Yes, we had a bag of your clothes brought over from South Dean. I trust they still fit after four years in France and a long illness.'

Well, that wasn't as dire a confession as he feared, Ben thought. In fact it was all very thoughtful. Mind you, they had rather assumed that his abduction was going to be successful, although he shouldn't quibble as they were acting in his best interests.

'Thank you for your foresight,' he said. 'I'm sure your grandfather's valet will be very helpful. My leg wound will need daily checking and re-dressing and he will be able to do it for me as well. Now that I am no longer Miss Bascombe's patient and she is no longer my nurse it will restore the proprieties as well.'

'Captain,' Laura said, 'as you say, we are no longer nurse and patient, so I think it is time you called me Laura rather than Nurse Bascombe which seems much too formal now.'

Ben smiled warmly.

'I shall be happy to call you Laura, provided, of course, in return you call me Ben.'

'Certainly … Ben,' a beaming Laura answered.

Lady Bascombe looked from one to the other and back again with a slightly smug smile.

'Very well,' she said. 'In that case, I am determined not to be left out. Ben, you may consider me to be an honorary aunt, so from now on, please call me Aunt Cecily.'

'Aunt Cecily, I am the one who is honoured.' He bowed slightly from his chair and Aunt Cecily nodded approval.

The door opened and an elderly gentleman stood there dressed all in black except for a white wing collar shirt.

'Ah, Thompson, do come in please, this is Captain Richards whom you will be assisting,' Cecily said, indicating Ben.

'Good morning, sir,' Thompson said with a short bow as he rapidly appraised Ben and his uniform. 'Will you be wishing to change for lunch?'

'Yes, indeed,' Ben replied as he pushed himself to his feet with the aid of his walking stick.

A little later, Laura joined her aunt in the upstairs drawing-room, next to the dining-room. She was wearing a simple royal blue dress with a fine lace bolero on top. Her hair had been brushed out and fell in natural waves.

Ben appeared with Thompson hovering behind him. Ben was dressed in a well tailored grey three-piece suit. It still fitted him well and the baggy styling of the trousers didn't show the bandage.

Ben and Laura looked at each other appreciatively as they sat down.

Laura cleared her throat.

'Ben, there is a little more we should confess as well.'

Ben raised his eyebrows speculatively as he wondered what else they might have done. It was starting to feel as they were taking control of his life.

'You did say you would stay with us if I took proper care of you,' Laura said with a slight tremor in her voice.

Ben nodded, slightly wide-eyed. Yes, he had agreed, but what else had she done?

'Captain Fellowes said your estate was going to rack and ruin. You've had enough problems without that, too, so we went to have a look.'

'I had a note from Potter to say that they were all coping and he was looking forward to my return. Was that not true? Or was Jeremy, Captain Fellowes, excessively pessimistic?'

'Captain Fellowes was mostly correct, but Potter is mostly correct too, now that we've provided some assistance.'

'Assistance?'

'Yes. Your gardener went into the village and recruited a couple of boys as assistant gardeners. There are quite a few children who have just finished school and need employment, you understand.

In the same way Mrs Green has taken on a couple of girls to train as maids.

'Then Aunt Cecily's steward, Mr Jennings, lent you a couple of horses and men for a week or so to help with the crops. Mills, my driver, also found a couple of wounded soldiers who were fit enough to help bring in the crops too.'

'Goodness, you have been busy. Where was my land steward while you were doing this? Why hadn't he taken charge?'

Laura pulled a regretful face.

'I am afraid, Ben, that he absconded some time ago and took the household cash with him.'

'What? He did what? I hope Potter sent the police after him. Why wasn't I told?'

'He did report it to the police. However, because of the war, the police are thin on the ground at the moment and, frankly, nobody has any idea where he went. The chance of catching him is negligible.

'Nobody told you because you had just been wounded in France and didn't need even more bad news on top of everything else.'

The reminder of 'everything else' gave Ben a slight pang of heartache, but he made an effort to stay focused on what he was being told.

'The miserable devil! If I ever catch sight of him he'll know all about it. How has everybody been coping in the meantime?'

'With difficulty. Potter, Mrs Green and the gardener have been dipping into their savings and making good use of produce from the kitchen garden.'

'What? But what about all these extra staff you've been hiring? How are they being paid?'

'You have it exactly. I've been hiring them and I'm paying them.'

'I don't understand.' Ben sat and stared, uncomprehending, at Laura.

'My grandfather left me more money than I know what to do with. This way, the money is doing something useful. Consider it a loan. Once the estate is back up and running again, no doubt it will be profitable and you can pay me back.'

'I'm shocked,' Ben said, 'about how so much has been going on and I knew nothing.' He stared into the distance. 'It's as if you've taken over while I wasn't looking.'

'No!' Laura said hurriedly. 'You mustn't think of it that way. It's just that I discovered my new friend was in difficulties, so I lent a helping hand. Isn't that what Captain Fellowes did by keeping an eye on you? I expect you would do the same for a friend or neighbour, too.

'Just as soon as you are fit enough, you must take charge again and put everything in order exactly the way that you want to. We've just kept it all going for a short time while you were incapacitated.'

Silence fell as Ben absorbed what he had been told and the ladies waited to see what he would say.

The quiet was broken by the butler announcing that lunch was served.

Laura took Ben's arm to steady him as they crossed to the dining-room where a cold collation had been set upon the table. They said nothing until they were seated at the table with food on their plates.

'Forgive me if I sounded ungrateful,' Ben said, 'but it's all been a surprise to me. What you have done is a kindness which I didn't expect from people that owed me nothing and who didn't even know of me a few weeks ago. I must thank you and I am greatly in your debt.'

'Ben,' Aunt Cecily replied, 'the whole country is in the debt of our soldiers who are risking much more than money, so you owe us nothing. You should view this as no more than the actions of good neighbours.'

'After lunch,' Laura said, before Ben could take issue with her aunt's comment, 'I suggest you take a little nap as you must be tired. The doctor said that over the next few weeks, you should take some regular, gentle exercise interspersed with rests until you get your strength back.

'After the nap we could take a turn in the garden, if you wish? You may have more questions for me when you've had time to think it over. Then, perhaps in a few days, when you feel up to it, we could motor over to South Dean and see how everyone is getting on?'

Ben nodded agreement.

'I must admit that I feel drained although I haven't done much today.'

* * *

A couple of hours later, Ben walked slowly through the house to the garden door, still wondering about the turn of events. Once outside, Laura took his arm, as much to reassure herself as anything that he was steady, while Ben used his walking stick in his other hand.

'I must say, Laura, I am still amazed at the amount you and you aunt have been doing for me. I mean, a few weeks ago we were complete strangers to each other and yet it seems you have been spending your time, and your money, too, on looking after my home as well as myself. Forgive me, but why?'

Laura walked in silence for a few self-conscious moments as she gathered her thoughts.

'After grandfather died, I was at a loose end, not knowing what to do with myself. Then I heard about volunteering at the hospital and I suppose it seemed like a continuation of caring for grand-father and past time I helped with the war effort, too.

'It was something to do which was almost familiar while I worked out what I really wanted to do with my life. I liked to think that Grandfather would have approved.

'Then I was put in charge of you and told in blunt terms it was up to me whether you lived or died. I can't half-do something — it had to be all or nothing, so I was determined that you live. It sounds perverse, but I was grateful to your cousin who annoyed you enough for you to gain the will to live.

'After a while I found you mattered to me and I couldn't send you home to a house which was going to be falling down around you. That would only unravel everything I thought I was managing to do.'

They walked on in silence as Ben absorbed what Laura had said. At last he stopped and turned towards her.

'I hardly know what to say. I was a stranger who had lost nearly everything and you owed me nothing, yet you are giving me back my life. To call it kind and generous is a wild understatement. I don't know how I will ever be able to thank you enough.'

Laura looked at him as she bit her lower lip. She knew already how she loved him and the only thanks she needed or wanted was for him to love her. But she couldn't say that. She gave him a wry smile.

'Perhaps it would be wise to inspect South Dean before you get carried away.' She turned them back to the direction they had been walking and tugged his elbow to start him walking and stop him talking.

Welcome Home

'Ben, if you are still feeling fit shall we go to South Dean this morning as we discussed yesterday?' Laura asked at breakfast.

'Certainly — it's about time I showed my face, although Potter knows where I am if there was anything urgent.'

'I'll come as well, if you don't mind,' Aunt Cecily added. 'I'd like to see how Mrs Green is getting on.'

By the time they had finished their breakfast, Mills was at the door with the car. It didn't take long for them to get to South Dean and as they motored slowly down his drive, Ben looked around.

Laura was relieved to see the drive was now weed free, and the grass had been cut.

Mills drew to a halt in front of the steps leading up to the front door. The door had opened and Potter was now hurrying down them to assist his new master.

Mills opened the car door and Potter

took Ben's hand to help him down on to the gravel of the drive as Laura came around from the other side of the car.

'Welcome home, my lord,' Potter said.

Laura looked sharply at Ben.

'My lord?' Ben looked at Laura, clearly puzzled.

'Well, yes. You knew I was Viscount Linton now, didn't you?'

'No, I did not. I thought you were Captain Benedict Richards, and nothing more.'

'Oh. I see. I suppose it never arose in the conversation, but surely the hospital ... ?'

Laura was miffed that nobody had mentioned that he was a peer, and glared at Ben.

'Well, perhaps they never said,' Ben continued lamely.

'Might I suggest that we go indoors?' Aunt Cecily interrupted. 'Then you two can quarrel in comfort while I have a cup of tea.' She headed up the steps and Laura joined her, leaving Ben to take the arm of his butler.

As they entered the house, Mrs Green came from the back, hastily removing an apron.

'Good morning, milady, miss,' she said with a curtsey.

'Good morning, Mrs Green,' Aunt Cecily replied. 'We've brought Captain Richards, or I should say, his lordship, to see how everything is.'

Mrs Green leaned a little sideways to see Mr Potter assisting Ben up the steps. Her eyes widened slightly to see how stiffly her master was walking.

'Would you ask Cook to do a tea tray for one of the downstairs rooms, and another for you and me in your parlour? You can let me know how you're getting on while Mr Potter brings his lordship and Miss Bascombe up to date.'

'Of course, your ladyship, right away,' Mrs Green said, before hurrying back the way she had come.

Laura opened the door to the small downstairs reception room as Ben walked in, leaning on Potter to one side and his walking stick on the other. Cecily observed this, before turning and finding her own way to Mrs Green's parlour.

Ben sat on an upright chair as usual and hooked his cane on its back. As Laura followed him into the room, he went to rise again.

'Oh, don't be silly,' she said. 'For goodness' sake sit down. I think we can dispense with the niceties for now. For that matter, would you take a seat as well, Potter.'

Mr Potter hesitated, clearly feeling that it was inappropriate for him to be sitting with his employers.

'Come, come, Potter, do take a seat, otherwise we shall get a crick in our necks looking up at you.' She looked at Ben for confirmation, who nodded.

'Now Potter, we've been keeping his lordship,' she narrowed her eyes at Ben, 'mostly in the dark about our efforts to resurrect the house and estate. I wanted him to concentrate on getting well and not fret about what he could have been doing here.'

A young, wide-eyed, somewhat frightened looking girl in a maid's uniform appeared in the doorway, holding a tea tray.

'Come in, Daisy, and put the tray on the side,' Potter said. 'You may pour the tea yourself and then bring the cups over to us.'

Ben turned a questioning eye to his butler.

'New, isn't she?'

'Yes, my lord, those of the maids who didn't succumb to the flu ran off before they could catch it.

'Now the epidemic has passed us by, Lady Bascombe asked Mrs Green to hire a couple of school leavers, like Daisy here, and train them as maids.'

Daisy placed a cup in front of Laura and a second in front of Ben. Potter gave her a nod of approval and she looked relieved.

'One for Mr Potter as well, please, Daisy.'

Potter opened his mouth as if to protest, but closed it again without speaking. They waited while Daisy gave Potter his cup before placing the sugar bowl and a plate of biscuits in the centre of the table.

Potter gave Daisy another slight nod of approval. She picked up the tray and left the room, looking pleased with herself.

Ben peered with interest at the biscuits and Laura, with a slight smile, pushed the plate closer to him. In the last few weeks she had learned that he had a sweet tooth.

'Now, Mr Potter, please tell us how everything has been going,' she said.

Couldn't Live Without You

Once he had rested a little and been brought up to date, an amazed Ben agreed to a short walk with Laura in the gardens, partly for the exercise, partly to see how things were for himself and partly to thank her again for all she had been doing.

'Laura, I can't begin to …'

Ben was interrupted as Claude sprang out in front of them from behind a hedge. He was holding a revolver.

'Where the devil have you been?' he snarled. 'The hospital said you'd been discharged and I've been hanging around here for ages wondering where you had gone.'

Laura clutched at Ben's arm and shrank a little behind him, before straightening up and moving back beside him. He put out an arm to stop her going nearer to Claude.

'I was a guest of Lady Bascombe, since you ask,' Ben replied. 'I suppose you've come to shoot me, have you?'

'Oh, well guessed,' Claude said. 'I suppose the gun is a clue.' He waved the gun a little to emphasise his point. 'Since you obviously didn't drink the tea or the gin, I have to be more direct, don't I?'

'Well yes, shooting me is likely to be more effective, but not if you wave it around like that.'

Claude pointed the gun at Ben instead of gesturing with it.

'I'm very sorry, Lady Bascombe, but obviously I'm going to have to shoot you too, since you'll be a witness.'

'Oh, no, I'm not Lady Bascombe,' Laura said.

'You're not?' Claude frowned. 'Who are you then?'

'I'm Miss Bascombe.'

Clause sighed impatiently.

'Well, never mind who you are, I'm going to have to shoot you anyway.'

'Claude, old chap,' Ben said, 'just before you shoot us, do me a favour, will you?'

'A favour? I don't know about that —

what do you mean?'

'I was wounded on the battlefield because the German army couldn't shoot straight. Then I spent several very painful weeks in hospitals and being dragged around. It was terrible and I really don't want to do that all again.

'When you shoot me, I need you to do it properly and kill me instead of just wounding me. To do that you'll have to come closer, otherwise you'll just be wounding me and that will be bad for both of us.'

'Why would I be wounding you instead of killing you? You're easily within range of this gun.'

'Because, dear cousin, your hand is trembling and there is no knowing what you might hit. Then there is the recoil and the bullet might go anywhere. If you come closer, you can be sure of hitting me.'

Clause looked puzzled at this advice but glanced at his hand and saw, yes, his hand was trembling. He was nervous and the gun was getting heavy. He moved closer.

'Yes, much better,' Ben said, 'but closer still please — look at the way your hand is still shaking.'

Claude moved a bit closer and looked down at his quivering hand. As he did so, Ben brought his walking stick up sharply and knocked the gun from Claude's hand. A shot rang out as the weapon went spinning into the hedge.

Ben brought the stick back down on the side of Claude's head and Claude stumbled sideways on to the ground. Ben threw himself heavily on to Claude as Claude started to get up. Ben yelped with pain when he fell awkwardly and Claude pushed him away.

'You beast!' Laura cried, rushing up to grab Claude who scrambled backwards out of reach. 'Why can't you leave him alone?'

Claude stood up, turned and ran off through the garden.

'You're a horrible man and I hate you!' Laura shouted, but didn't try to chase him. She kneeled on the ground. 'Ben!

Ben! Where are you hurt?'

'It's my leg again,' he said through gritted teeth.

'He didn't shoot you?'

'No, no, it's just my leg.'

'Thank goodness for that,' Laura said. Ben looked up at her with a pained expression on his face. 'Well, it could have been worse! We can fix your leg.'

An out-of-breath old gardener appeared from the shrubbery, quickly followed by a young apprentice. Then in short order appeared a puffing, red-cheeked and plump Potter, a limping Mills, and Lady Bascombe, accompanied by Mrs Green the housekeeper.

'Mills,' Ben said, 'there's a Webley revolver in the hedge somewhere. Find it and take it out in case he comes back for it. Use a cloth so you don't get fingerprints on it and give it to Potter to put somewhere safe. You,' Ben said, pointing to the gardening boy, 'do you know where the police station is?'

'Yes, sir, your honour, milord,' he said.

'Good. When Mills has found the

gun, go with him to get the police. Mrs Green, please go and heat some water and find some bandages, I think I have pulled my stitches,' Ben said, pointing to his leg where a bloodstain was showing through his trousers.

Aunt Cecily gasped and then she, Laura and the gardener helped him stand. He put his arms across the shoulders of the gardener and Laura and they half carried, half dragged him to the house while Cecily went ahead to open the doors.

They went into the nearest room as one of the new maids came with towels to put on the sofa.

'Get a pair of scissors,' Laura said to the girl, who scampered off to find some. 'We're going to have to cut your trouser leg to see what has happened,' Laura said to Ben as they eased him on to the sofa.

'Yes, fine,' he said, trying not to wince as they lifted his leg, 'this pair is horribly out of fashion anyway. Thompson said they were only tolerable because they fitted easily over my bandage.'

A short while later, Laura, Cecily and Mrs Green stood back to survey a fresh bandage on Ben's calf. The bloodstained ruin of his trouser leg hung around the bandage.

'My lord, shall I make up a room for you?' Mrs Green asked.

'I think, Captain, it will be easier for all of us if we take you home for now,' Cecily said. 'It's not far and we are already organised to look after you. That way, Mrs Green can finish setting your house to rights while you recuperate.'

Ben, whose lips were pressed together due to the pain, nodded his agreement.

'In the meantime, Mrs Green, please ask Cook to make a cup of tea for everybody,' Cecily continued.

As Mrs Green turned to leave the room, Potter appeared in the doorway.

'The police constable is here to see you, milord,' he announced.

The constable came in with his helmet under his arm as Cecily followed

Mrs Green out of the room.

'Good afternoon, sir, I understand there was an incident earlier. Perhaps you could tell me about it.' He drew a notebook and pencil from his breast pocket.

★ ★ ★

A little later the constable was being returned to the police station, complete with the revolver, by Mills. Ben and Laura were quietly drinking a second cup of tea when Laura's cup suddenly started to rattle on the saucer.

Ben took it from her hands and put it on the coffee table as Laura's face contorted with distress and she started crying. He pulled her into his arms and she sobbed uncontrollably into his shoulder.

Ben held her tightly and made soothing noises as he rubbed her back.

'Hush now, it's all over, he won't trouble us any more.'

'I really thought he was going to kill

you this time and when you told him to come closer I was so scared.'

'I know, I know, but you were very brave. I worried you might do something sudden and make him panic. I had to get him to come close enough to me so I could hit the gun with my stick.'

'I was too petrified to do something sudden.'

'I was hoping that even if he shot me you would have a chance to run away. Thank goodness we didn't have to find out.'

'If he had shot you I wouldn't have run away, I would have attacked him with everything I had. '

'We might have both been shot in that case.'

'It wouldn't have mattered. I wouldn't have wanted to live without you.'

Ben lifted Laura off his damp shoulder so that he could kiss her tenderly. Tenderly quickly became passionately and Ben suddenly forgot the pain from his leg.

Meanwhile, Aunt Cecily and Mrs Green were settled in Mrs Green's parlour.

'Don't you think we should be doing something?' Mrs Green asked.

Aunt Cecily considered for a moment. She had a shrewd idea that Ben and Laura would appreciate being left alone for a while. She shook her head.

'No. Miss Bascombe has experience of nursing the captain. He is no doubt battle-hardened and can cope with any stress. I expect they will appreciate a quiet interlude to compose themselves.

'Mr Mills will soon be back from the police station. The gardener's boy is probably thrilled with all the excitement and with riding in the motor car. Potter and the gardener are sitting down in the kitchen with Cook and probably having a little chat.

'The villainous Mr Legge has run away and will be apprehended once word gets around. No, I don't think there is anything we need to do for the moment.'

By the time the ladies had started on their second cup of tea, Ben had hoisted Laura on to his lap and they had stopped kissing for a moment.

'Laura,' he said, 'I don't wish to live without you. When I thought you were Daniel's wife, I was quite desolate. I dreaded the idea of staying under Daniel's roof when I was in love with his wife.'

A smile spread across Laura's face.

'After you kidnapped me and then my worst fear evaporated, I felt jubilant,' Ben continued. 'When you told me you had kidnapped my house here at South Dean as well, I wasn't sure if I should be relieved or worried that my life was spinning out of control.

'I think the only way for me to stop feeling dizzy would be if you would marry me, so that I have some idea of what you will do next. Will you marry me, my love?'

'Somebody needs to look after you and I don't want it to be anybody but me, so yes, I will.'

There was a knock at the door and

Ben put Laura back on to the sofa beside him.

'Enter!'

The door opened to reveal Potter.

'Excuse me sir, but Mills has returned with the car.'

'Very good,' Ben said, 'but first would you ask Lady Bascombe to come and see me with Mrs Green, cook and yourself.'

The four of them arrived in short order with Cecily at the front. She looked as if she was suppressing a smile.

'I hope you will excuse my not standing in the circumstances,' Ben said, 'but I wish to tell you I have asked Miss Bascombe for her hand in marriage and she has accepted.'

The others offered their congratulations from faces wreathed in smiles.

Ben turned to Laura.

'Is there somebody of whom I should be asking permission?' he asked quietly.

Laura patted his hand.

'By the time we get married it will be no longer necessary.' She rose to accept a kiss on her cheek from Aunt Cecily.

'Aunt Cecily, do you think we should go and see Daniel tomorrow? After all, he is the head of the family now.'

'Yes, that would be all that is proper but I have no doubt he will be pleased for you.'

Dearly Beloved ...

The church was full. Ben stood at the front with his best man, Jeremy. He turned to survey the congregation as they waited for the bride.By now he could recognise most of his new family. Aunt Cecily sat in the front row with cousin Mary and the very young Viscount Bascombe between them.

Behind them were Aunt Agnes and Aunt Phyllis. Cousin Ernest was sitting next to the aunts with a young lady that Ben didn't recognise. She had heavy, uninspiring features and was wearing what looked like an expensive mink coat.

Next to them was cousin Norman with his fiancée Miss Schuster, and then cousin Walter at the end of the row.

The music started and Ben only had eyes for his bride as she came up the aisle on Daniel's arm, followed by Grace and Prudence. Ben and Laura smiled at each other before turning to face the vicar.

'Dearly beloved, we are gathered here

today in the sight of God to join this man and this woman in holy matrimony ... If any person here can show cause why these two people should not be joined in holy matrimony, speak now or for ever hold your peace.' As the vicar made the customary pause, he looked over their heads to where there were the sounds of a scuffle at the back of the church.

'Because he's going to be dead!' a wild-looking Claude cried, running up the aisle brandishing a revolver.

Ben pulled Laura behind himself to protect her from the madman. Jeremy then stepped in front of them both. Before Claude got to the front, he went crashing to the floor, rugby tackled by Walter.

The gun went off, the shot echoing around the church before the gun went clattering along the floor to be picked up by Jeremy. Claude was then pounced upon by Norman and Daniel.

Claude was dragged away ranting and raving by several ex-soldiers who were now employees of the Elmhurst estate.

★ ★ ★

Some time later, the meal was over, the toasts were said and everyone repaired to the large sitting-room. A string quartet in the corner had just finished tuning their instruments. Ben turned to Laura.

'Some time ago I said you were being absurd. You had told me to find a nice girl and marry her, I should invite you to the wedding and then you would dance with me. I was wrong to say you were absurd because I did and here you are. Lady Linton, may I have this dance?'

Epilogue

Once again the family were gathering in the drawing-room at Compton Park, just over a year from the reading of the late earl's will.

The earl's portly solicitor was once more standing behind a table upon which rested several sheets of paper. This time the family were not dressed in black and Laura was sitting beside her husband.

Once all the family were seated and their chatter had died down, the solicitor also sat, cleared his throat and picked up the sheaf of papers.

'My lords, ladies and gentlemen,' he began, 'the late earl left me extensive instructions covering a wide range of possible outcomes during the year just past.

'Now that I have had written reports from all of the beneficiaries I am able to follow those instructions.

'I confirm that the house in Littlehampton is to be made over to Agnes,

Lady Weston, without any further require-
ments or obligations. Similarly the house
and estate at Elmhurst Manor are given
to Cecily, Lady Bascombe.

'To my grandsons Norman and Walter I leave a further two hundred pounds
with the hope that they will continue to
act wisely. To my granddaughter Laura
who has followed my instructions and
found a husband worthy of her I leave
another five thousand pounds.'

This was much more than Laura had
expected and meant that they would
now have the capital to modernise the
estate at South Dean.

Due to the war there was a shortage
of able-bodied men. They knew mod-
ern machinery which could be operated
by less fit men would be the answer, but
they had lacked the money to pursue the
idea. Now they could buy machinery,
hire more wounded ex-soldiers and put
the heart back into the land at the same
time.

The solicitor was still speaking.

'To all of my grandchildren, other than

Laura and Daniel, I leave two hundred pounds in trust until either they marry or reach the age of thirty-five. The residue of the estate I leave to my grandson Daniel.

'My lords, ladies and gentlemen, that concludes the will and wishes of the late earl. I shall be writing to each of you in due course. I thank you for your time and patience. Good day to you.' He stood and swept the papers into his briefcase.

Other titles in the
Linford Romance Library:

PROMISE OF SPRING

Beth Francis

After the breakdown of her relation-
ship with Justin, Amy moves out of
town to a small village. In her cosy
cottage, with her kind next-door
neighbour Meg, she's determined
to make a fresh start. But there are
complications in store. Though Amy
has sworn never to risk her heart
again, she finds her friendship with
Meg's great-nephew Mike deepening
into something more. Until Mike's
ex-girlfriend Emma reappears on the
scene — and so does Justin . . .

DATE WITH DANGER

Jill Barry

Bonnie spends carefree summers in the Welsh seaside resort where her mother runs a guesthouse. But things will change after she meets Patrik, a young Hungarian funfair worker. Both she and her friend Kay find love in the heady whirl of the fair — and are also are fast learning how people they thought they knew can sometimes conceal secrets. As Patrik moonlights for one of her mother's friends, Bonnie fears that he may be heading into danger ...

ROSE'S ALPINE ADVENTURE

Christina Garbutt

Rose is in need of excitement. Taking a leap of faith, she flies to the Alps to take up the position of personal assistant to Olympic ski champion Liam Woods. Though she's never skied before — or even spent much time around snow — that's not going to stop her! But she hadn't bargained on someone trying to sabotage Liam's new venture ... or on her attraction to him. Can she and Liam save his business — and will he fall for her too?

A BODY IN THE CHAPEL

Philippa Carey

Ipswich, 1919: On her way to teach Sunday School, Margaret Preston finds a badly injured man unconscious at the chapel gate. She and her widowed father, Reverend Preston, take him in and call the doctor. When the stranger regains consciousness, he tells them he has lost his memory, not knowing who he is or how he came to be there. As he and Margaret grow closer, their fondness for one another increases. But she is already being courted by another man . . .

BLETCHLEY SECRETS

Dawn Knox

1940: A cold upbringing with parents who unfairly blame her for a family tragedy has robbed Jess of all self-worth and confidence. Escaping to join the WAAF, she's stationed at RAF Holsmere, until a seemingly unimportant competition leads to her recruitment into the secret world of code-breaking at Bletchley Park. Love, however, eludes her: the men she chooses are totally unsuitable — until she meets Daniel. But there is so much which separates them. Can they ever find happiness together?